SWEET TREATS

CHOCOLATE

2021

ROMANCE
WRITERS
of Australia

Chocolate 2021 Sweet Treats Anthology

Anthology of Short Stories published by Romance Writers of Australia

Inc © 2021

eBook format: 978-0-6485877-9-8

Print format: 978-0-6485877-8-1

Sweet Treats Coordinator: Paquita Fadden

Cover design by Louisa West - Bookcoverology

Edited by Pam Collings

Formatting by Kim Lambert

OTHER SWEET TREATS ANTHOLOGIES

Cupcake 2020

SWEET TREATS

CHOCOLATE

Short Story Anthology

2021

TONI D'ALIA	CORDELIA FOX
ARIETTA RICHMOND	STEPHANIE ASHTON
FRANCES DALL'ALBA	CAROLINE DENESS
LOUISA DUVAL	AMY HUTTON
KYLIE JACOBS	J A MACNALLY
FIONA MARSDEN	CLARE MILES
VALERIE MILLER	GEORGIA MOORE

KRISTIN SILK

CONTENTS

FOREWORD

Sweet and delicious, decadent, beautiful chocolate.

Fifteen stories, with chocolate at their core. Who could resist?

Epic love stories, and gossiping grannies.

Second chances at love and old crushes.

From the depths of time to the reaches of outer space.

Young love, mature love, and everything in-between.

Every story here has love and sweetness.

Every story will capture your heart and make you love the couples and their sweet tooths.

So, grab your chocolate, be it a bar or block, whether it be solid or liquid goodness, and settle in to enjoy our newest Sweet Treats Anthology - Chocolate.

Tracey Rosen

I
SWEET DREAMS
TONI D'ALIA

Coco's hand shook as she held a blade covered in chocolate buttercream frosting. She glanced up at the large timer. The numbers were ticking over quickly. She took a deep breath and let it out slowly, trying to calm her nerves. She'd been making cakes and sweets for most of her life, but never had she felt this kind of pressure. Then again, she'd never competed on a national television show for a chance to win a large cash prize and a publishing contract for her very own cookbook. This was the final challenge in the competition, and if she won, all her dreams would come true.

She gently spun the board under the cake, resting the blade on the top of the sponge to smooth the icing. It had been one of the first baking tricks her mother had taught her.

"There's just two minutes left," the show's host announced. "Make them count."

Coco looked over at Kit Masters who stood at the bench next to hers. He smiled as he sprinkled icing sugar over a chocolate souffle he'd just pulled from the oven. His shoulder length black hair was held back by his trademark blue bandana, and as usual, he looked to be in full control of his kitchen. She was both impressed and infuriated that he always seemed so composed during filming, and she couldn't help but wonder if he ever felt nervous or unsure of himself.

She shook her head and quickly returned her attention to the dish in front of her. She opened the door of the small fridge under the bench and pulled out the bowl of chocolate mousse she'd made. Making small scoops with the mixture, she placed them strategically on the top of the cake.

"One minute left," the host called out. "This is it. The whole competition comes down to this one moment. It's your last chance to add any finishing touches to your dish."

She picked up the plate of chocolate curls she'd made earlier and scattered them delicately over the top of the cake.

With thirty seconds left on the clock she had just enough time to pipe some of the mousse around the base of the cake.

"And ten, nine, eight, seven..." the host, along with a crowd of eliminated contestants, called out. The camera crew zoomed in and out capturing the final rushed moments of each contestant.

Coco wiped the edge of her plate making sure the presentation was perfect.

"Three, two, one, and that's time!" the host announced.

Applause filled the room and Coco smiled as she looked at her chocolate dessert. It was exactly as she'd imagined, and win or lose, she was happy with what she'd produced. She just hoped she'd done enough to win this challenge.

She looked over at Kit and found him staring back at her. She held his gaze for a moment before looking down at the bench, her cheeks turning red. As much as she wanted to, she just couldn't work him out. He'd been so friendly when they'd first met at the beginning of the competition, and she'd been attracted to his easy-going nature and wicked sense of humour.

But after a few weeks, he'd started acting aloof and indifferent when he was in her company and Coco had no idea what had caused the change in him.

She left her position behind her bench and walked towards the centre of the room where the judges waited patiently. When Kit joined her, she shook his hand and smiled up at him. A shiver ran up her arm when they touched, and she pulled her hand away quickly, breaking the connection. Despite being thrown together for months of countless cooking trials, interviews, and eliminations, she was no closer to understanding him, and yet she was drawn to him. He intrigued her and she couldn't deny the way her heart beat faster when he was near, or the thrill she felt when he smiled at her.

Cameras surrounded them and the judges tasted and evaluated each of their dishes. So much was riding on this result. Coco could barely breathe. She could see the judges' mouths moving but there was a roar in her ears that was getting louder and louder, preventing her from hearing what the judges were saying. She plastered a smile on her face and focused on her breathing. She felt sweat form on her palms, and she tried to wipe them discreetly on her apron.

Kit stepped closer to her, and his hand brushed against hers.

She looked up at him and found gentle brown eyes staring back at her.

"Breathe," he whispered.

She took a deep breath and let it out slowly.

The host smiled into the camera positioned in front of her. "And we'll announce the winner right after this short break."

"Cut," a member of the crew called, and the room relaxed.

"Are you okay?" Kit leaned close and whispered. His breath on her ear made her heart race and she swallowed the lump in her throat. She looked up at him and tears filled her eyes.

"I don't know. I feel a bit faint," she admitted as the room began to spin.

Kit acted quickly, placing his arm around her waist for support. He was solid and strong, and Coco felt at home in his arms. "We need a chair and a bottle of water, please," he commanded, "and get the medic."

Coco looked up at him, surprised by his attentiveness.

There was a flurry of activity as people rushed around them. A chair was produced as if from thin air, and a bottle of water was shoved into her hand. She sat down and took a couple of sips of the cold water. A medic appeared and quickly placed a material cuff around her upper arm to take her blood pressure.

"You're okay, Coco," the medic told her. "I think you just need to take a break for a few minutes. Lay down, drink some fluids, and we can get back to recording when you're feeling up to it." He led her to a small room, and she laid on the couch. "Take some small sips of water and lay on your side. You should feel better soon. I'll get someone to sit with you."

"I can stay with her," Kit said from the doorway. He walked in and grabbed a chair from the table, dragging it closer to the couch. "I mean, if Coco wants me to."

The medic looked at Coco. "Is that okay with you?"

Coco nodded.

"Lovely. Thanks, Kit," the medic said as he walked out the door.

Kit sat down next to her. "Are you feeling better now?"

She smiled weakly, embarrassed at having caused a scene. "Yes, I am. Thanks for your help, Kit."

"It was nothing," he said.

She closed her eyes and rested her head on a soft pillow.

"It's a lot of pressure, isn't it?" He paused for a moment before saying, "Did you think it would be this stressful when you signed up?"

Coco sighed. "Not in a million years."

"Me either," he said, leaning back on his chair and stretching his legs out in front of him.

"It's been a good experience though, hasn't it? I can't believe that was the final challenge."

Kit looked down at his hands resting in his lap. "So, what will you do when the show finishes?"

Coco smiled. "I want to open a café but..."

"But?"

"I'm a little cash-strapped at the moment. If I win, my plan is to use the prize money to get it off the ground." Coco told him about the small cosy café she'd always pictured, with a large range of chocolate desserts and sweets on offer. There'd be an eclectic mix of chairs and tables, and colourful art on the walls. It would be a place to bring loved ones for special occasions and celebrations, a place to make memories or to remember good times, a place with lots of heart.

"That's a sweet dream, Coco," he said, smiling.

"What about you? What are your plans?" she asked.

Kit thought for a moment. "I'd like to keep experimenting and pushing culinary boundaries. I want to create desserts with new and exciting flavour combinations."

"You'll be great at that, Kit," she said. "Your chocolate brownie layer cake was genius. You've made some really amazing dishes during the competition."

"Thanks. You have too."

Coco smiled at the compliment.

It was just like they were back at the beginning of the competition, when they had been easy in each other's company. Coco knew time was running out if she wanted to find out why he had changed. After the winner was announced they'd go their own ways, and she might never see him again.

She closed her eyes and took a deep breath. "Kit, can I ask you something?"

He looked at her warily.

She took a breath and released it slowly. "Did I do something to upset you?"

Kit frowned and shook his head.

Coco sat up and turned to face him. "Then what happened? I mean, when we met, I thought you liked me, but—"

"I do like you," he said softly.

Coco gasped. "Kit, be honest. Until today, you've barely tolerated me."

Kit looked down at his lap.

"You know I like you Kit, but I really wish you'd just tell me the truth." She let out a heavy sigh as Kit shook his head.

A movement in the doorway caught her attention. A lady holding a clipboard shuffled anxiously from foot to foot. "Excuse me, but if you're feeling up to it, we need you two back on set."

Coco sighed again. "Well, if you do like me, you have a funny way of showing it." She stood up and marched back to her position on set. She obviously wasn't going to get to the bottom of it and it broke her heart. She'd miss him when the show ended.

Kit caught up with her as they reached their marks. "Are you feeling okay now? Do you think you're going to faint again?"

Coco rolled her eyes.

"I didn't actually faint last time, but I'm fine now thanks."

"Look, Coco," he said, his eyes staring into hers, "can we talk after filming has finished?"

Coco nodded, a hopeful spark igniting in her heart. "Sure," she whispered.

"Ready?" a crew member asked.

Coco took a deep breath. It was time to find out whether her baking dreams were about to come true. This was it.

"And – action!"

CR80

Coco felt numb all over. She couldn't believe what had transpired in the last hour. Confetti and streamers had fallen from the ceiling as the host announced the winner of the show. Cameras filmed everything, but it was all a blur from the moment her name was called.

She'd won. She'd actually won. Tears filled her eyes as she signed the contract that would allow her dreams to come true. She scribbled her name on the papers in front of her, and it was official.

"Congratulations, Coco," Kit said as she entered the hallway. He'd taken off his blue bandana, removed his chef's coat, and stood leaning against the wall, waiting for her.

"Thank you, Kit. I can't believe it."

"I can. You're very talented."

She blushed. "So are you."

Kit looked down at his feet. "Um, Coco, I was wondering if I could maybe take you out for a coffee or something. I mean, if you want to?" He kicked at the floor gently as he spoke, his hands shoved into his pockets.

Coco tilted her head to the side as she looked up at him. This was a completely different side to him; one she hadn't seen during filming. He'd always appeared so confident and self-assured, but now... "I'd like that, Kit."

He looked up and met her eyes. "Great. There's a little place nearby that I'd like to show you."

Coco nodded and together they walked outside into the sunlight.

C3&O

Their table was covered with plates and bowls. It had been a true chocolate celebration, with chocolate pudding, chocolate covered strawberries, chocolate-chip pancakes, and chocolate sundaes – Coco's favourite desserts.

The little restaurant was not far from the studio and sat on the ground floor of an old building. It had big windows that looked out at the busy street.

"That was delicious," she said, giggling as she wiped her mouth with the serviette. "This place is amazing. Thanks for bringing me here." She felt so relaxed in Kit's company, and she wished it had always been like this.

Kit smiled. "It's one of my favourite places in the city. My grandfather brought me here once a month when I was little. He'd let me pick anything I wanted on the menu. He taught me to experiment with flavours and tastes. It's one of the reasons I love cooking." He fidgeted with the cutlery on the table. "I thought you'd like it here."

Coco reached out and placed her hand on top of his. "I love it. It's sort of what I'd like to do with my café."

"So, you think you'll go ahead with your plan to open a cafe?"

Coco nodded. "Absolutely. There's so much to do and I'm not sure where to start, but I'm so excited."

"I'm really happy for you."

Coco looked down at the table for a moment before raising her eyes to meet his. "Kit, can you tell me why you changed during filming?"

Kit sighed heavily. "You said you wanted honesty, right?"

Coco nodded.

"Well, the truth is..." he whispered, closing his eyes for a moment, "the truth is I do like you. I like you a lot."

Coco looked at him in disbelief. "Then why—"

"I knew pretty quickly that you and I would end up in the final. You're so talented."

Coco shook her head. "But I don't understand."

"I was worried the competition might come between us if we started something during filming. I wanted to wait until the show was over to tell you how I felt, but it was getting harder to hide my feelings for you so I thought it would be easier to stay away."

Coco sighed. "I wish you'd told me."

Kit shook his head. "Me too. You don't know how hard it was to hide what I was feeling."

"Oh, I think I might have some idea. I like you too, Kit," she said.

"You do?"

Coco nodded. She looked up at him and took a deep breath. "Kit, this might sound crazy, but why don't you come help me set up the café. Better yet, start it with me."

"Like partners?"

"Yes. We'd make a great team. You could create whatever desserts you like and experiment as much as you want to. This would be the perfect job for you. You'd get to do exactly what you love."

Kit reached out and took her hand in his. "Are you sure? The café is your dream."

Coco nodded. "I'm sure. My dream is big enough for two. Plus, you'll get to do what you've always dreamed of doing too. With both of us there, it's sure to be a success."

Kit smiled. "I think you're right. We'd make a great team, in and out of the kitchen."

"So, you'll start the café with me? You'll be my partner?"

Kit nodded and moved his chair closer to her. "I'd love to."

Coco grinned. "To our sweet future," she said, as she put her arms around his shoulders and looked into his eyes.

He leaned in and kissed her gently, before whispering, "And to sweet dreams."

2

TWENTY-SIX LETTERS

CORDELIA FOX

T he story of how my father fell in love with my mother is the shortest love story in the world. At least, it is the way he tells it.

I saw her dancing in her blue dress and I was a goner. I knew she was the one for me. And it turned out she felt the same way.

That's it. Beginning, middle and end. In three sentences.

It's to the point; it does have that in its favour.

It's terribly unsatisfying, though. Like biting into a summer apricot; round and full of promise, but floury inside, dry, and juiceless to the very stone. Technically it's still an apricot, but it's a poor excuse for one. It's a fruit that should hang its head in shame. If it had a neck.

Mum's version is quite different. It starts like this.

Well, you know how romantic your father is.

Uh, no. I don't know. He keeps his cards pretty close to his chest, my dad. I wouldn't have described him as romantic, not by any stretch.

> *He spent a good twenty minutes eyeing me up as I danced by. You know how I love to dance.*

Yep, I know that all right. She taught the four of us to dance. She was always shimmying around the house, her records turned up full blast. It was embarrassing, especially when we had friends over.

> *I spotted him as soon as he arrived. He was difficult to miss. Tall, dark, and handsome, just like the story book princes.*

> *I didn't let on that I'd seen him, of course. Your father took his time but once he saw me flirting with Robbie Jenkins, he made his move. He asked me to dance, and afterwards he bought me a cocktail. A Bees Knees.*

He bought it for her because he thought she was the bee's knees, obviously.

I made one the other day. Two ounces of gin, three quarter ounces of honey syrup, half ounce of fresh lemon juice. Shaken together with ice. Yummy.

> *Your father didn't rush me. He knew I wasn't keen to settle down. Actually, I was a bit of a one for the lads. Fresh out of Teachers' College, full of energy and enthusiasm, I just wanted to have fun. It was the sixties after all.*

> *Desmond was the serious, steady type. I was too young and giddy to recognise the worth of those qualities in the beginning. But he won me over in the end.*

Now we get to the interesting bit. Dad is serious, like she says, but he's got hidden depths and he's surprisingly creative.

> *I was teaching the new entrants and your father knew how much I loved getting the littlies into reading. I suppose I talked about it a lot; how I wanted to foster their imagination through a love of words.*
>
> *He didn't say much, but he was listening. Away he went and hatched up the most beautiful, dreamy plan in the whole world.*

She's right. It was an exceptional plan.

> *I didn't really have any idea what it was going to become. Not at first. It seemed like a pretty standard gesture. A box of chocolates.*
>
> *But the first bite – oh my. I'd never tasted anything like it in my life. Luxuriously rich swirls with tiny pieces of slivered almonds. I've always had a sweet tooth, and in particular a weakness for chocolate. Your father knew that.*

Dad's friend, Rupert, was a chocolatier. Only an apprentice chocolatier at the time but he was good.

No surprise he's famous now.

> *I can still taste them. Dark and delicious. Just like Desmond turned out to be.*

As kids we used to hate the secret look of satisfaction that appeared on her face at this point in the story.

We'd shout, "Ooh Mum, that's gross!"

Now I think it's sort of cute.

> *But that wasn't the best part. Oh no. With the box was a piece of card. Thirty centimetres by thirty centimetres. Old-fashioned parchment-like card, wrapped in tissue paper. Your father had drawn an 'A' on the card. Alongside it was the word 'Almond' and the loveliest drawing of an almond tree that you ever did see.*

It's a stunning drawing. Like I said, my dad's creative. If he ever gave up building, he could make a career as an artist. Dominic's the one who inherited Dad's creativity gene. His song lyrics are pure poetry.

> *He turned up a few weeks later with another box. I'd finished all the almond chocolates by then and I was delighted to be getting more. I'd half expected that he'd turn up with some B-flavoured chocolates. I was expecting blueberry or blackberry.*
>
> *This time, not wanting to look greedy, I opened the card first. You can imagine my surprise when the card was B for Buttons.*

When I tell people this story, I always ask them what they think the B-chocolates will be. No one has ever guessed Buttons. Who would?

> *I must confess I was a bit let down. I was looking forward to more sweet treats but there's no such thing as button-flavoured chocolate. Desmond told me later, much later, that he'd seen my face fall and could barely hold back his laughter. As you know, he's a bit of a joker, your father.*

Mmm. Dad used to spin us the most outrageous stories when we were small.

I'd gone through a phase of refusing to get in Dad's double kayak, for his weekend fishing trips with Mum and me. To get his own way he convinced me that unicorns lived in the fjord, in an underwater kingdom. I spent hours gazing down into the depths hoping to catch a glimpse of their silvery manes.

I was pissed when I found out it was all a lie.

I hate lies.

> *Anyway, I tried to hide my feelings. He'd gone to the trouble of bringing me a present and I didn't want to be rude. Good manners are very important. You'd do well to remember that.*

Yes, Mum.

She's a real stickler for manners, my mum.

> *I studied the picture so I could get over my disappointment and, what does Dominic always say? It blew me away.*

> *Desmond had drawn a handful of buttons, and each one was unique. A different colour, size, and shape. There was even a button in the shape of a teddy bear.*

> *Your father had seen me sewing teddy buttons on the jumper I'd knitted for Thea's first born and he'd drawn an exact replica. He never misses a trick.*

He *almost* never misses a trick. He didn't notice what was happening to Kate. None of us did.

It's me who's most to blame. I'm the big sister, the eldest. I should have known.

Then I opened the box.

Inside there were chocolate buttons. Not those awful things that you get inside Easter eggs, all exactly the same. These were individually crafted buttons, just like Desmond's buttons. They were almost too pretty to eat.

Your father wouldn't tell me where he'd got them from – not at first. I didn't meet Rupert until much later, but as you know he has a gift for chocolates.

That's an understatement. Rupert is a Chocolate Wizard.

By the time your father gave me the letter C, I'd gone on a few dates with him. Not many though. He was often away, out of Montreal, doing building work. If there was work to be had, he'd disappear.

I didn't mind. I was busy with my own life. Montreal was a big, exciting city, especially for a country girl like me. I loved it. I was never bored. Mind you, only boring people ever feel bored.

That particular line formed the song sheet of our childhood.

It annoyed us all, but it drove Ben absolutely wild; probably because he's ever so slightly boring. Not that I'd ever tell him. For a boring person he's got an evil temper.

Your father turned up with a large box, much bigger than the previous two. It was wrapped in brown paper and tied with an orange ribbon.

I couldn't resist opening it before the card. You'll never guess what it was.

I don't need to guess. I know what it was.

But you don't, do you?

> A massive, stripy ginger-orange cat, made of cake. I took a photo of it and insisted that Desmond sit down and eat it with me in the sunshine.

> It was only then that I opened the card. It wasn't C for Cat, as I'd expected. It was C for Le Chat.

> Your father was always teasing me about my appalling French. It was all very well for him, growing up in Quebec with French speaking parents. I only learned French at high school.

Mum actually speaks passable French now, but it was Dad and Grand-mère and Grand-père, who made sure that we could speak both languages.

Dad always reverts to French when he's emotional. When I told him what Kate's husband had done, he didn't speak English for a week. But enough of that. You're here for a love story.

> It took me days to finish eating the cake and I thought that was the end of that. ABC – a lovely gift for a teacher. I took the cards to a print shop in the city and had copies made so I could put them up in the classroom.

> The original drawings were too special to take to school. I put them in a box wrapped in tissue to keep them safe.

Just so you know. That wasn't the end.

It wouldn't be such a great love story if it stopped there, would it?

Just saying.

It was at that point that I went away.

*On holiday, that is. To Vancouver to stay with my
cousin. I was there for a month. And when I got back
your father appeared with the letter D.*

This part of the story makes me uneasy.

A month is a long time and Mum never says what she
got up to on that holiday. We've tried to get it out of her,
but she always changes the subject. Dad won't talk about it
either.

Ben and Dominic think Mum had a secret boyfriend,
but Kate and I reckon something really bad went down.
Something that could have wrecked Mum and Dad's
relationship.

I hate secrets, even more than lies. They fester, like an
infection simmering under the skin. Sometimes I wonder if
Mum's secret is like that.

Happy, shiny facades can hide a lot of ugliness. Kate knows
all about that.

*That's when it became clear that Desmond had
decided to court me. He wasn't stopping at C. He was
going to make all twenty-six letters. He'd planned to
draw me an alphabet frieze.*

That's pretty up there, right? It shows some downright
dedication to the long haul. Twenty-six is a big number. Maybe
not over a lifetime, but for a courtship, it's massive.

Twenty-six is some pretty serious wooing. But like I said, my
dad's a serious sort of guy.

The letter D was so romantic. It was D for La Danseuse, dancing girl. Your father had drawn me dancing in my blue dress. The one I'd worn when we first met. What can I say? I was moved. I still am.

And the chocolates, they were so cute.

Little white chocolates in the shape of high-heeled shoes, covered in sprinkles. I sat on your father's knee, feeding him shoe after shoe. One for him, one for me. He said we were a real pair.

Cheesy, huh? We had a lot of fun with that one, as kids. We'd ponce around the house in Mum and Dad's shoes, offering each other shoes to nibble, and laughing ourselves to bits. Dominic always grabbed the best shoes, and often one of Mum's dresses as well. Even as a little boy he was a performer. Ben reckons he was born for the stage. A born show-off, I say.

It took more than a year, but your father brought me a card for every single letter of the alphabet, and with each card he brought chocolates. I tried to play it cool, but who could resist the romance of that?

When Desmond was away working, and I was missing him, I would unwrap the cards and spread them out on the bed all around me. Just to feel him close.

And she thinks Dad's the romantic one.

But I bet you're wondering about the letters.

Don't get me wrong, I loved the chocolates, but it was your father's drawings of the letters that touched my heart.

*The children at school loved them too. They were
so excited when I brought each new one into class. I'd
hand it around so they could look at it up close. They
were only copies, of course. I kept the real ones safe.
We'd talk about the word on the card, and I'd make
up a story to go with it. Oh, it was lovely.*

Mum did the same thing with us when we were kids.

The storytelling bit. We had copies of the twenty-six
letters on our bedroom wall. When we were teenagers – Ben,
Dominic, Kate and me – we'd choose a letter and make up the
rudest story we could, using as many words as possible
starting with that letter. Kate peed her pants once, she
laughed so hard.

*I'll tell you the letters, and the chocolates. I know
them off by heart.*

*E for Egg. They came with a box of chocolate
eggs.*

*F for Les Fleurs. Flower-shaped chocolates, each
a different flavour.*

G for Galaxy. Chocolate stars.

*H for Hen. A hen that fitted in the palm of my
hand, carved out of solid milk chocolate.*

*I for Les Immigrants. A chocolate cake in the
shape of a suitcase.*

*J for Jalapeño. A bag of chilli-spiced hot chocolate
powder. Wonderful on cold mornings.*

*K for Kayak. Two carved chocolate paddles. By
that stage Desmond had bought a double kayak and
he'd take me out on the fjord with him.*

I told you Dad was obsessed with kayaking. Actually, we all are. Probably because we spent half our childhood out on the water looking for unicorns.

> *L for Love. Oh my. That's what life is all about. Love. It really does make the world go around.*

> *By that stage in the alphabet I was already deeply in love with your father.*

> *I knew he was the man for me. He'd shown me his love in so many ways but to see the card, with the drawing of him and me symbolising love, well, it doesn't get any better than that.*

Actually, it does get better. We still haven't got to the best bit.

> *M for Maple. Maple syrup flavoured chocolates. Rupert's made a fortune exporting these. The Prime Minister called them the pride of Canada. Imagine that.*

> *N for La Neige. Snowflake-shaped white chocolates.*

> *O for Orange. Wickedly strong Cointreau liqueur chocolates.*

> *P for Phoenix. The most beautiful bird carved out of dark chocolate, surrounded by tiny orange flame-shaped chocolates.*

> *Q for Queen. A chocolate crown with edible gold and silver jewels.*

> *R for Le Raisin. A bunch of chocolate covered grapes.*

> *S for Salmon. Fish-shaped chocolates, complete with scales.*

> *T for La Tisane. Chocolates in the shape of teacups.*

> *U for Unicorn. White chocolates with silver sprinkles.*

I hate unicorns.

That's Dad's fault.

When I was ten, I went through every story book in the bookshelves, looking for pictures of unicorns. Then I got the biggest, fattest black pen I could find and scribbled over every unicorn horn.

Mum went completely berserk when she found out. To her, books are holy objects.

> *V for Venus. Heart shaped chocolates. This was the second box of heart chocolates. The first came with L for Love. They were white chocolate. These ones were pink.*

> *W for Worm. A bag of chocolate worms.*

> *X for Le Xérès. Sherry flavoured chocolates.*

> *Y for Les Yeux. Two chocolate eyes, complete with eyelashes. Pretty and very tasty.*

> *And finally, Z for Zanzibar. Chocolates flavoured with the spices of Zanzibar. Vanilla, black pepper, cinnamon, nutmeg, ginger. Simply delicious.*

Here's the best bit. The thing that lifts this love story above all the rest.

A secret message.

> *You'll never guess what happened when your father gave me Z.*

He pointed to a very small letter in gold, hidden in the drawing. It was an E. I asked him what it was for, but he just tapped the side of his nose. You know how he does.

Yes, I do. It's an infuriating habit.

Ben does it too. It's part of his whole arrogant lawyer vibe. Brothers. Can't live with them, can't live without them.

I made guesses and pestered him and made more guesses, and eventually he told me that I had to search for the hidden message.

I spread all the cards out on the floor, in front of the fire. It was winter and we were drinking mulled wine while we ate those lovely, spiced chocolates. Anyway, I examined each one, very carefully. Desmond said I should start at A.

I discovered the letter M hidden in the branches of the almond tree, then the letter E on one of the buttons on the B card.

I got a pen and paper and wrote each one down as I found it.

When I read the message, well I have to confess, I was a bit teary. There was no decision to be made, of course. I was madly in love with your father. I still am.

My answer was yes. It couldn't be anything else.

But what was the message?

That's what you want to know, isn't it?

Here it is (with punctuation added).

Meg, mon amour, will you be my wife?

A marriage proposal in twenty-six letters.

Told you it was a good story.

3
THE SCENT OF FIRST LOVE
ARIETTA RICHMOND

The scent wrapped around her as soon as she stepped through the door.

Chocolate – a specific blend of chocolate, which she had not thought to ever experience again.

It was the scent of her childhood; the scent of first love.

The bittersweet scent of what might have been.

The door fell closed behind her, and she stood, caught by the memories, eyes closed, breathing it in.

In that moment, she was sixteen again, back in Napoli, standing in the sun in front of their neighbour's shop. Before her stood Marco – Marco, only a year or so older than her, whom she had loved all her life – holding out a silver cup, from which that scent drifted.

"Try it" he said, "Father has been experimenting with new flavours."

She took the proffered cup, a sharp tingle of awareness heating her body as her fingers brushed his, and lifted it, allowing the rich, treacly-thick substance within to slip into her mouth, leaving a sticky droplet poised on the edge of her lip.

As she savoured the taste, Marco reached out, and brushed that droplet away with his fingertip. She had felt that touch as if it had been a kiss. He had turned away then, suddenly unwilling to meet her eyes. After that, she had hoped...

But nothing had come of her hopes, and, two years later, she had been swept off her feet by the handsome English cloth merchant who had come to trade with her father, and married him. She had loved him, without doubt, and had three wonderful children to show for it – but he was near eight years in the grave.

That thought brought her sharply back to the present, where she stood in the front-of-shop of Morton Empire Imports. Mr Manning and Mr Jenkins must wonder if she was quite mad, to be standing there like a fool.

She opened her eyes.

And blinked, certain that she must be hallucinating.

Before her, a man had turned from the counter, where it seemed that he had been speaking with Mr Manning. He held in his hands a silver cup, which might well have been twin to the one she had been remembering, and it was from that cup that the scent of chocolate rose. But what took her breath away was his face.

He seemed as frozen as she for a moment, and then, his voice just a little shaky, he spoke.

"Sophia...?"

It did not matter that thirty-three years had passed, or that the voice of a boy had matured into that of a man – she would have known it, instantly, anywhere.

Marco Giannis had come to London to begin a new business, leaving his shop in Napoli to his son. His wife was dead these ten years, taken by God, along with the babe she had been trying to birth at the time. Staying in Napoli had become less and less appealing, and the idea had taken root that, now that Leopold had married, it was time for Marco to leave.

He had chosen London for all sorts of supposedly rational reasons, all the while knowing, in his heart, that he had come here because this was where Sophia had gone, all those years before.

Sophia had been much in his thoughts of late. It was not that he had not been happy in his marriage – it was simply that memory glossed things in a golden haze, which left him regretting that he had never spoken to Sophia of his feelings, back when they were both so young.

So he had come to seek out, after some research, a business which might be suitable to partner with him in the establishment, here, of a chocolatier, where he might purvey his family recipes and the new chocolate products he had developed recently. He required a partner with funds to invest, and with the right connections to source all of the exotic spices and flavours he needed and wanted, to carry out his vision.

In Italy, ever since the destructions wrought on trade by the Napoleonic wars, he had been less able to find sources of those items he needed, even seven years after the end of the wars. Here, he hoped that things might be different.

Morton Empire Imports, in whose storefront he now stood, had been recommended to him by a number of people – its owner was, apparently, the richest merchant in London, and had, some years before, been ennobled. The possibility of a business partner with direct connections to the nobility, as well as the wealth to permit the scale of operations he wished for, was most appealing.

When the place had been mentioned, the name had seemed vaguely familiar – now he knew why.

Now, the past snapped back into sharp focus. Morton... the name of the man who had swept Sophia out of his life, the name he had, he suspected, intentionally chosen to forget, as a result. Was it he who had been ennobled? Did he still live?

Impossibly, in his eyes at least, she seemed barely to have changed, although it had been more than three decades. He had turned, leaving the small samovar like stove on the countertop, and frozen in place with the cup in his hand, enraptured by the sight of her. After some moments, he found his voice.

"Sophia...?" It was not that he was unsure; more that he did not know if she would wish to acknowledge him. She swallowed, and nodded. An odd sense of childlike mischief rose within him, and he extended the cup. "Try it" he said, "I have been experimenting with new flavours."

It was instantly obvious that she remembered, and his heart beat harder at that realisation, a little flutter of joy beginning deep within him.

She took the cup, and brought it to her lips. The chocolate was cooling, the liquid becoming thicker, and, as it had that day so long ago, a droplet stayed on her lip. For a moment, as the richly textured chocolate filled her mouth, she closed her eyes, as if savouring something far more significant than a simple mouthful of chocolate, however exquisite its compounding. Then those dark eyes opened and met his.

He reached out, ever so slowly, and brushed that droplet from her lip. She turned her head and touched his fingertip with a featherlight kiss. Her voice, when she spoke, was like sunshine after rain, bright and full of everything he had not known he needed.

"Marco. That flavour is not so new... whatever small refinements you may have made, it is somehow the same. It will forever be the taste of a summer afternoon in Napoli."

He knew that he grinned like a fool, but, as she held out the cup, he simply took it, and bowed.

She stepped forward, and he turned back to the rather startled gentleman behind the counter, who Sophia was now addressing.

"Mr Manning, what have you been discussing with Signore Giannis?"

"Mrs Morton, Signore Giannis has brought us a business proposal – one which, I must say, I thought might interest you."

"I see. Manning, I ask that you grant Signore Giannis every assistance in whatever he may require. If this proposal has anything at all to do with chocolate, as I rather suspect it does, then, whilst I will wish to negotiate the best agreement for Morton Empire Imports, I can tell you now that I will, if at all possible, move forward with the proposal that he brings to us. And, as Gabriel is currently out of London, that decision will lie wholly with me."

"Certainly, Mrs Morton."

Mr Manning met Marco's eyes, his expression curious, and Marco nearly laughed at the absurdity of it – that his Sophia had become so assertive, so well respected, so powerful – he was delighted – and very curious himself – for a start, who was Gabriel? That had certainly not been the name of the man she had married. And, if she was 'Mrs Morton' then it was not the man she had married who had been ennobled.

She turned to him again, and that smile lit her eyes.

"Marco, if you are free to do so, I would ask you to dine with me this evening at eight, at Morton House, so that we might discuss this proposal of yours in detail. Manning can provide you with the direction."

What could he say but yes?

"I would be delighted, Mrs Morton."

He bowed again, and she moved to leave, but as she passed him, she spoke in a near whisper.

"From you, Marco, I prefer Sophia."

CRBO

As the carriage transported her the short distance to Morton House, Sophia felt oddly detached, as if she were suspended somewhere in place and time, caught between that long ago day in Napoli and now, connected only by the scent of chocolate.

Despite that distance, her mind still processed normal things in the background, deciding what she should ask Cook to prepare for dinner, what she should wear, and what she wanted to ask Marco – not just about his business proposal, but about his life. Perhaps, if she knew more of his life in the intervening years, it might all seem more real.

He had changed so little!

Yes, there was now some grey in his dark hair, as there was in hers, but little else was different – he had not run to fat, as a man who worked with rich foods might have been expected to do, and he moved with the same smooth certainty that she remembered. Suddenly, she was impatient – the evening could not come soon enough!

The carriage drew to a halt, and she startled the footman by almost springing down the steps, then bustled into the house. The odd detachment was gone – all that was left was anticipation, and the lingering taste of chocolate.

CRBO

Marco rapped the door knocker, listening to its echo come back to him from inside the large and impressive house. He smoothed his coat, nervous – more so than he had been for many years – and it was not a feeling he liked. But, more than that, he was curious, and, if he was to be honest with himself, a little afraid.

That flutter of hope which had risen within him, back in the shop – was it about to be utterly crushed? Was he about to discover that Mr Morton still lived? He had gained the impression, in the shop, that the gentleman was not about – but was that false? Not that he would wish any man dead, but... part of him clung to the idea that his Sophia might be free...

He almost laughed at himself then – 'his Sophia' – how very presumptuous of him that thought was. But having thought it, he could not unthink it – in all of the ways that mattered, regardless of what had filled the years in between, she would always be 'his Sophia' – the girl who had captured his heart in Napoli, when he had been too unsure of himself to tell her of his feelings.

The door opened, and a rather cheerful looking footman regarded him. He offered his calling card. The man glanced at it and nodded.

"Signore Giannis, please, come in. I will show you to the parlour, then let Mrs Morton know that you have arrived."

"Thank you." Marco held out the small parcel he carried. "Please take this to the kitchens - it is chocolate, from my latest batch."

The footman bowed, took the parcel, and turned.

Marco followed him, and stepped into the parlour, where his attention was caught by the four paintings which hung along the opposite wall, above the mantel. They were all family portraits. The first showed a woman, obviously Sophia, a man, who was alike enough to his memory of the Englishman for him to believe him the man she had married, and three children – two boys and a girl.

He swallowed, wondering in that moment if she had been truly happy with her choice.

The next showed a man who had enough of Sophia in the lines of his face to likely be her son, accompanied by a woman with rich mahogany toned hair, who was holding a small boy.

The following one showed a young woman, who was so like Sophia had been, in Napoli, that it was as if time had been turned back – she was accompanied by a man whose hair was so fair as to be like polished spun gold, and she also held a small child.

The final one showed a man who must be Sophia's other son, with a young woman, who was as fair as he was dark. He contemplated them all, his curiosity reaching fever pitch – he had to know more of her life.

"They are good likenesses, I think. My husband commissioned the first one, when business began to be good enough to afford it. The others were painted only in the last few years – by my daughter by marriage, who is a talented artist." Sophia stepped past him and went to indicate the woman in the final picture. "Primrose hated painting herself – she said that trying to study oneself in a mirror while posing was nigh on impossible."

She laughed lightly, but there was an edge to it, as if she too felt nervous. He swallowed, and went to her. There was only one way to know. He had to ask.

"Sophia…" She turned, her eyes meeting his. "Your husband…?"

Her eyes clouded for mere seconds, as if with sadness, then she gave a little shake of her head.

"Gone to God, Marco, nigh on eight years ago now." There was a hesitation, then she continued, her voice softer, "And you? Did you marry?"

"I did. But Giulia is also gone, ten years ago. I have a son – Leopold, who married, and now runs the shop in Napoli – but no other children." He felt the grief again, of all those lost babes – those born too early, those who had lived only short lives. "No other children, though we tried – and she died with the last one, on the day that should have been its birthday."

Sophia reached out then, and cupped his cheek in her hand.

"Then I have been blessed, by comparison. I quickened only

the three times – but they all lived, and live still, and are happy. My daughter is a Duchess, my older son ennobled as an Earl, and I have grandchildren, and will soon have more."

He pressed a kiss to her palm, then captured her hand in his.

"Blessed indeed. Yet – there is something in your voice – you sound... not joyous..."

They were, he realised, speaking in Italian – they had done so, from the first moment that she had entered this room – with her, it seemed only right. Her fingers tightened on his.

"That is a good way of putting it. I have respect, wealth, comfort, friends, and family who are wonderful, yet – I am lonely, I think, now that the children are all married and living their own lives. I have thought of the past more often of late, and wondered what might have been, wondered what had happened to all those I knew. When I stepped through the door today, and the scent of your chocolate wrapped around me, it was as if the years had disappeared. I almost thought you a ghost – until you spoke."

"I felt much the same, for a moment. I knew that you had come to London, all those years ago, and I hoped... but I never imagined that I might see you again."

She glanced up at the paintings for a moment, and he wondered what thoughts went through her mind, but was chagrined to realise that he did not, now, know her well enough to understand the fleeting expressions which crossed her face. Then she brought her eyes back to him, and granted him a smile which dazzled, and sent his heart racing, that flutter of hope becoming as a storm of wings within him.

"Marco... I choose to say to you, now, what I should have said that afternoon in Napoli so long ago, when I did not have the courage or confidence to speak. I loved you then, even though I was barely old enough to understand what that meant and, even though I loved my husband and treasured the time that we had together, I find that I love you still, that the years do not matter. I am sorry that I did not tell you then, how I felt. If I had..."

"...if you had, then things might have been different, for both of us. For I loved you then, and also lacked the courage to speak. When the Englishman swept you away, I regretted my hesitancy – but by then, of course, it was too late. I loved Giulia. I would not have married a woman I did not care for – but in love, there are degrees..."

The sparkle of tears made her eyes bright, and he pulled her to him gently. She stepped into his arms, and he bent his lips to hers, tasting that which he had dreamed of for all his life, for the first time. He knew, then, with utter certainty, that he wanted more than a business partnership from this woman. He spun her around, and they moved a little apart, breathless.

"Marco..."

"Sophia... marry me? Please – let us begin again, as if we were still young, as if our hesitation had not cost us all those years."

For a moment, he thought that she might refuse, until she brought her lips to his, and whispered, "Yes," before kissing him deeply.

A tap on the door broke them apart.

"Mrs Morton, Cook asks how she should prepare the chocolate which Signore Giannis brought?"

Her eyes met his as she replied.

"With love."

4
BREAKING THE RULES
STEPHANIE ASHTON

I f there was a word for feeling simultaneously excited and petrified, Simone Collins couldn't recall it. She looked at her reflection in the mirror, her eyes drawn to her initials in the logo on her chocolatier's apron. She lifted her chin, kept her eyes on her face and mouthed the words she'd been practising for ten minutes.

"Hi, Morgan." She poked her tongue out at her reflection. "Oh, hi, Morgan." She emphasised her former girlfriend's name.

Simone rolled her eyes and shut up. This was ridiculous. And it was equally stupid to think that what she had with Morgan Prohasky before Morgan had left for Melbourne could mean anything. How could Simone compete now that Morgan was the AFL women's star player.

A long sigh escaped as she recalled Morgan's face. The Prohasky cheekbones, high with smatterings of freckles, had always made her think that this is what it meant to swoon. Not that she had ever been anything but the practical type. In the quiet of the evenings when she was baking, Morgan's blue-green eyes framed by long, dark lashes had returned to her daydreams. Since Simone's mum announced the national women's football team were playing a round for the bushfire appeal, memories and a racing heartbeat had reignited.

No, I've never been married. Nearly, but just not the right person. Simone stopped forcing her smile. All those nights in high school thinking of Morgan. It had been over between them a long time ago. She'd stopped wondering and moved on. If only she'd had the courage to do something about Morgan when she had the chance. She would never have caused Matt and his family so much pain.

"Mumma."

Her two-year-old daughter interrupted her thoughts, reaching her arms out to her as she was brought into the bedroom by the perfumed, pristine Louise Collins.

"We've had a fun morning, haven't we, Mackenzie?" Simone's mum ran her hands over her tailored, shirt.

"Thanks for looking after her, Mum. I'll get changed and come help with dinner. I dropped a whole bowl of brownie mix on myself this morning."

"Oh here." Simone picked up the white gift box off her queen-size bed. "Would you like some double dark chocolate coconut brownie off-cuts? I'm thinking of adding them to the menu as 'cut-ies'. What do you think?"

"Thank you, darling, that sounds delicious and – interesting." Her mum turned to leave with the box. She paused. "Is Matt coming for dinner tonight?"

Reality returned. Simone reached out to take her wriggling daughter in her arms, lifting her into the air, waiting for shrieks of laughter before bringing her back down to the plush carpet of her parents' home, their home for the time being.

"No, not tonight. He's asked for Mackenzie to visit on

Wednesday; it's his mum's birthday."

"Are you planning to go watch the AFL women's game this weekend?" Her mum's gaze remained steadfastly in her direction and leaned onto the door frame. Mackenzie waddled over to the mirrored wardrobe behind them.

"I'm not sure yet, Mum. I was thinking of going with Lauren and her new boyfriend. It looks like it'll be fun," she added hopefully.

"It's the team the Prohasky girl plays for," her mum continued. Her tone smoothing to a monotone.

Breath caught in her chest, Simone turned away, busying herself unnecessarily with the scatter of cushions and toys on her bed.

"No, Mackenzie, leave it please," she raised her voice, retrieving the silver teardrop pendant from her bedside table as chubby fingers reached it.

"Mum, if we end up going, would you mind looking after Mackenzie for a couple of hours?"

Louise Collins pushed herself off the doorframe, arms still folded. "I'm not sure I want you to see her again. Remember what happened last time." Her mother gave a half-smile, uncrossed her arms, turned on her heel and padded down the long hall.

"Mum," Simone called after her, forcing her voice to be cheerful. "It's just a football game."

That was Mum, never one to go out of her way when it came to Morgan Prohasky. She still couldn't even say her full name.

There were moments in Morgan's life she knew instantly she'd replay in her head several times. Looking into the home crowd from the Summerton football ground and locking eyes with Simone Collins for the first time in six years was one of them.

Morgan let the hot water run over her tanned, toned shoulders. The comforting warmth of the shower cubicle gave her the solitude she needed to replay the moment over again. The steamy change rooms were noisy.

A few minutes into the second quarter, Morgan positioned herself close to the goals, and for a reason she'd not been able to determine, she looked to the crowd at her right. As their eyes locked, she couldn't bear to move away from that familiar face. Simone Collins smiled straight at her as if the last six years hadn't passed. She still wore her straight blond hair in a high ponytail. A wave of emotion slammed into Morgan at the realisation there was barely fifty metres between them.

"Morgan, are you done yet?" A teammate pounded on the cubicle door, not waiting for a response.

In the solitude of the shower cubicle Morgan smiled as she recalled seeing Simone again. She'd tried hard for everyone: her parents, the football club, her coach, to focus only on what mattered to them. Until this point, she hadn't allowed herself the time to stop and realise how much she'd sacrificed.

"Get out of the showers, you lot. We've got celebrating to do!" Another cheer went up from the team as Coach Johnson's voice from the club room next door boomed.

When the final siren blared, Morgan turned back to the fence. She looked up and down the fence line but couldn't see Simone's large blue eyes or that stunning smile.

Perhaps she's never forgiven me for leaving. Perhaps I should have stayed in Melbourne.

Morgan switched off the taps. With energy she usually reserved for the final quarter burst of fight, she ran the towel over her body and pulled her team tracksuit on before tying a grey hoodie around her waist.

"Prohasky, where are you going? Get back here! Your dad will be starting his speech any minute." Coach's voice sounded behind her as she swiftly manoeuvred towards the club room entrance. She looked at her phone. She had ten minutes to find Simone. No, make that nine.

⚜

The sunshine sparkled off the Prohasky Family Club Room sign hung above its door. Simone stood against a corner pole of the veranda, sweating profusely despite being out of the direct heat of the afternoon. It seemed as though all of Summerton had descended on the club rooms for the fundraising match. It didn't seem to matter that it was the visitors who had won. But then Summerton had never forgotten the Prohaskys. Morgan may have well been playing for the Summerton Stars.

Simone nodded hellos to the locals she knew and avoided Matt Hudson's cousins who sauntered past, beer stubbies already in hand.

"Simone?"

Simone's stomach tightened at hearing the husky voice that was once so familiar. Morgan was here, in front of her again, finally. Smiling. Looking hotter than she'd ever remembered.

"Hi." For all her rehearsed words, her voice came out octaves higher than she'd planned. Her skin prickled, and the underlying passion swelled. "Congratulations. You were amazing out there."

"Thanks." Morgan's smile notched Simone's heart rate higher. "It's been a while, hasn't it?"

"Since we last saw each other? Yes." Simone noticed perspiration glistening on Morgan's cheekbones.

"What's news?" Morgan asked.

Weaving in and out of the footy club supporters, a bunch of shrieking kids ran past them.

"Slow down, you lot." Simone instinctively reached out an arm to ease their pace. "How long are you here for?" she asked Morgan, hoping the answer would give them more than these five minutes to talk. The footy club presentation and speeches would start soon, and she wasn't sure she'd be able to stand in the same room as Morgan for an hour without losing her mind.

"The team's here for five days. We've going to some charity events. Although we're at the dog show tomorrow and I'm not sure how that will help anyone. I've been asked to be a judge, can you believe?" Morgan laughed. "I mean, I love dogs, but can you imagine me picking a winner?"

"Ah, that would be a no." Simone laughed. "Well, all you need to know is that Hunter, the Malamute, is going for the championship with this win," Simone teased. "Ashleigh Porter – do you remember her? – she'll be all over you if she doesn't get it," she explained with a grin, her right hand signalling a slit to the throat.

"Ashleigh Porter? She hated me at school," Morgan groaned with a smile, rolling her eyes upward to the expanse of blue sky. "It sounds like I need a refresher in Summerton diplomacy. I thought I'd left all that behind." Morgan shivered, pulling the jumper from around her waist over her head.

"You did leave it behind. All of it." The words, the wrong words, spilled out before Simone had a chance to cut them off. And they suddenly felt like a big deal wedged between them.

She looked at Morgan's face re-emerging from her grey top.

Morgan reached out and touched Simone's arm. Their eyes locked. Her fingertips felt warm and smooth. Her movements slowed, focusing entirely on her hot skin under Morgan's touch. The thrum of the footy crowds around them seemed subdued.

"I did. You're right." Morgan's hand dropped from Simone's arm as she looked over to the presentation stage. The sun was blaring down on the officials' heads as mikes were tested. "I don't drink, but Dad tells me there are a few new places to try. Are you around later for a drink?"

"I'm baking tonight," Simone replied. If Morgan's presence wasn't messing with her composure, she'd have been able to quickly reply with a resounding 'yes'.

"Okay, no worries." Morgan crossed her arms.

"It would be great to see you. Honestly. It's my business, Coko. I bake, but mostly in the evenings," Simone explained.

"Ohhhh, okay," Morgan replied cautiously.

"I'm baking chocolate brownies tonight. I'll bring you some."

"Ah, no, chocolate is off the menu these days," Morgan answered, matter-of-factly.

"Totally off?" For three seconds Simone tried to contemplate a chocolate-less existence. She reflected on the neatness of Morgan's words. They matched the precision of her physique; not a hint of excess was evident.

"Just one of a few things I've given up." Morgan was only half-smiling.

"Let me guess. You gave up chocolate for footy?" Simone teased.

"You got it."

"Well, you'll just have to come and have a non-alcoholic drink in my kitchen and avoid having any chocolate. That'll be a test."

"I'm up for that." Morgan nodded, unfolding her arms.

"...the winning team's captain to the stage, Summerton's star, Morgan Prohasky," the voice of the home team's president sounded over the ageing public address.

"See you soon," Morgan called out over her shoulder as she was jostled towards the stage by the crowd. Simone began navigating her way through the crowds the other way. She had some work to do.

⊂ॐ১

"I could sit here and say how good it is to see you; how much I've missed you," Morgan said, the warm skin of her legs brushed up against Simone's under the cool Caesarstone baking bench in the Coko chocolatier's kitchen. "How I've never stopped thinking of you, missing you. But..."

"There's a 'but'?" Simone laughed nervously. It was hard to concentrate. She was grateful she could practically bake in her sleep. She wanted to reach out and touch Morgan, but she needed to keep a level head.

"But they're just words." Morgan paused. "What I'm really interested in knowing is – would you want to see me again?" Morgan's face focused on hers from across the wide cocoa-smeared table. Three years ago, those words from this woman would have melted Simone like chocolate left in her shop window on a stifling summer's day.

"I almost got married, Morgan." There was more Simone had to share; more that Morgan had to know. She scraped the chocolate down the sides of the mixer.

"That makes sense."

Simone couldn't tell if she was being serious.

"I'm surprised you didn't hear." Simone poured the brownie batter into the waiting baking trays.

"Yeah, Mum and Dad kept a lot of stuff from me, not just about you. They were trying to keep my focus on footy. Everything's about Aussie Rules, in case you hadn't noticed." Morgan let a wry smile emerge. "Which is handy when you're trying hard to forget someone."

Morgan turned her face to look at Simone. The words resonated.

I wish I'd known. Simone wasn't brave enough to let the words surface.

"Can I ask who you almost married?" Morgan spoke softly.

"Matt Hudson." Simone watched Morgan's eyebrows briefly rise, then lower.

"Do you want to tell me about it? Did you love him?"

"What's to say? He was hurt. His parents, my parents weren't happy. I thought it was love, yes."

"That's a lot about how other people are feeling. How are you feeling?"

Warmth emanated through her body. Simone smoothed out the brownie batter with the spatula, flicking her head towards the cluster of photos behind them.

"That's our daughter, Mackenzie. She's two." Simone smiled. "She's the best."

"You have a daughter?" Morgan raised her hands to her mouth, moving closer to the photos. Out of the corner of her eye, Simone was relieved to notice Morgan's smile. "Wow, you have a daughter. That is big."

"The biggest." Simone agreed, her chocolate brownie-smeared fingers reaching for the silver pendant at her neck.

CRRD

Simone looked out into the busy main street from behind her chocolatier counter. The afternoon summer sky shimmered brilliant blue yet again. The shop's air conditioning was doing its best to keep last night's batch of chocolate coconut bites, double chocolate brownies and choc-hazelnut-filled doughnuts intact. As she leant over the end of the glass counter to pull the window blind down a little, Simone's stomach plunged. The unmistakable stride of Morgan Prohasky was approaching.

Sweat broke across Simone's forehead, and she suddenly became acutely aware of her every movement. Whatever happened after Morgan made the next fifty metres to her, Simone knew it would be defining. She crouched under the counter, absentmindedly tidying stacks of her unassembled giftboxes. Their late-night conversation replayed in her mind. Had she said too much? Would being Mackenzie's mum be too challenging for Morgan? Simone took a deep breath and stood up. She looked right into the stormy blue-green eyes.

"I'd like a box of your Double Chocolate Brownies, please," Morgan stated calmly, her expression not betraying any emotion.

Simone's eyes widened. "Brownies? For you?" she stammered, staring at Morgan's wide smile.

"Yes, please. I'd like a box of those Double Chocolate Brownie Off-cuties," she repeated. "I think they're called cuties. I mean, I'm sure the full-size versions are just as delicious, but I've heard the brownies off-cuts here are worth breaking my strict, very strict footy player's diet for."

Simone swallowed purposefully and bit the inside of her mouth to keep the widest smile from escaping. She replayed Morgan's words over again and tried to slow her heartbeat as she reached under the glass counter and retrieved one of the giftboxes. She looked into Morgan's eyes and handed them over. Her fingers brushed against the warm hands waiting. A wave of tingles danced up her spine.

"It's a daily decadence that I think is worth getting in trouble for," Morgan continued, looking into the counter at the other treats. "If you're up for it, that is." Morgan looked at her.

"Daily? You're planning on having brownies daily? That's quite a change. Are you sure you're ready for this much chocolate?"

Simone clenched down on both sides of her cheeks now, barely containing her smile.

"Yes. Please," Morgan replied. "I wonder if you could deliver it to Melbourne sometimes."

Simone breathed out.

"Would that be okay, Simone?" Morgan asked reaching out to intertwine their fingers.

"It would be very okay, Morgan Prohasky. It'd be very okay." Simone walked the six steps from behind the counter to stand as close as she ever had to a customer.

"Maybe these should be called bruties?" Morgan turned to face Simone, her arm reaching around to bring her – and her chocolate floury mess of an apron – in close.

"Brooooties?" Simone repeated.

"Bruties. A mash-up of brownie and off-cuts," Morgan explained in faux-seriousness.

Simone groaned and smiled, her eyes crinkling with happiness.

"Come on, it's brilliant," Morgan teased, a grin finally spreading across her face. "You've got to admit."

"You're brilliant." Simone let Morgan pull her in even closer, her face within inches. Long moments seemed to pass as Simone took in Morgan's bluey green eyes and her full, chocolate brownie-smudged mouth. She lifted her hand and slowly slid the tip of a finger across Morgan's warm, parted lips. A delicious shiver erupted as Morgan leaned her cheek into Simone's hand. Simone paused, taking it all in before she let the space between them disappear and kissed her.

5

THE CHOCOLATE HEART

FRANCES DALL'ALBA

"Toby, what the heck? What do you mean you're double booked?" Jennifer's hands landed with a thump on her lap. A scowl replaced the smile she greeted him with only seconds ago.

"I didn't plan it this way. Okay, Jen?" Toby mussed his light brown curls as he sat down on the opposite side of her desk.

"But this weekend is vital!" Jennifer tapped the bundle of papers in front of her. "Our promotional prospects depend on us getting this presentation right and *you* have something else on?"

"Look, I'm with you all the way. This affects me too, but I have something else very important to do this weekend."

Jennifer wheeled her chair back and rose, making her way to the water cooler positioned outside her door. Three months on this thesis and Toby decided to renege now! She drank a mouthful of water and choked on it as it tunnelled down her throat.

"Are you okay?" Toby asked from her office.

"No, I'm not, but thanks for asking," was her blunt response.

How could he fail her now? They teamed up for this joint project because they worked so damn well together.

She gulped in some much-needed air while her gaze remained fixed on her busy co-workers. The success of this project was her pathway up the corporate ladder. Agreeing to partner with Toby had been the right decision. With his quick-witted intelligence and her driving passion, they got things done. She wasn't about to throw this opportunity away.

"I'd like you to come with me."

Jennifer's fingers curled around the paper cup she held, slowly scrunching it, before flinging it into the bin adjacent to the water cooler. This was not good. She'd ignored the fluttering of her traitorous heart whenever she was near Toby and prioritised her career over her heart. Safely ensconced in the friend-zone, she was used to being his sounding board every time a new girlfriend entered or left the scene. It had been months since the last one, but if Toby was putting a new girlfriend before *their* project, she would fry him! Her heart be damned!

She poked her head around the doorway and gave Toby the best evil stare she could muster. "If this involves some weird threesome with a new girlfriend, I will *never* forgive you."

Toby's jaw dropped as Jennifer re-entered her office. She leaned against the doorframe, folded her arms, and glared at him.

His dove-grey eyes blazed back at her. "Is that what you think I'd do?"

"Why else would you risk your career?"

"Christ, how are you reading me so wrong?"

She wrenched her gaze away from his and looked past his shoulder. She would deny that until she was blue in the face. She'd heard and seen it all. For three years she'd pushed her pathetic longings to the background and concentrated her efforts on working together to instigate friendly, healthy rivalry, vital for the growth of their careers. To fail at such a crucial point was not going to happen on her watch!

"I'm going to visit my nan. She needs me this weekend."

Huh? Jennifer snapped her attention back and stepped her way around Toby. She tripped and just managed to fall into her office chair. "Your *grandmother*?"

"Yes, my nan. Didn't you grow up with a grandmother?"

Whaaat? They'd discussed many things over the years, but this subject had never come up. "Er... ahh... actually, no I didn't."

Toby slumped over her desk. "You get two chances."

"Mum's parents died years ago and Dad's live in Turkey."

"Oh." Toby's gaze wandered over her face. "So that's where you get your great olive complexion from."

An embarrassing blush crept up her neck and she lost some of her fight. "And my non-existent height," she added.

"Oh, right, let's not start on that topic," Toby added with a chuckle.

Jennifer snorted. "Yeah, leave that one alone." His height jokes always scored a reaction from her.

Toby sat back. "So, this is the deal. We go to Nan's and stay until Mum gets back Sunday. After we put Nan to bed each night, we can practise our presentation."

"Isn't there someone else who can take care of her?"

Toby shook his head. "She's my nan and I like being there for her. Besides, she's getting on and needs a hand."

"She does?"

"Yeah."

Resigning herself to this change of plan, Jennifer asked, "Where does she live?"

"Three hour's drive away and I'm leaving Thursday afternoon. Roster a day off and come to work with your bag packed."

"But," Jennifer stuttered, "we can't leave that early!"

Toby rose and leaned over her desk. "Yes, we can. I already hinted to HR that you need Friday off."

"What?" Jennifer shot up. "You thought you'd have me convinced before asking?"

Toby raked a hand through his messy curls and sighed. "I was hoping so." Then he casually kissed her on her cheek before turning and leaving her office. "Thursday afternoon," he called over his retreating back.

Jennifer slowly straightened. Another heated blush rushed up her neck. Toby had only ever touched her with friendly gestures, so this kiss was out of the ordinary and had her pulse racing erratically. She gulped and willed her brain to function professionally. It was one weekend. The presence of one geriatric woman could not possibly change anything.

◌৪৪৩

"Good morning. Jennifer, isn't it? Come and have some breakfast."

Jennifer walked into a cloud of delicious smelling pancakes and saw a petite grey-haired woman by the stove. They arrived too late the previous night for introductions. "Good morning, Nan. Is it okay if I call you that? Toby said I should."

"Of course, dear, everyone does." She smiled.

Jennifer inhaled the mouth-watering aroma just as her stomach grumbled. "Is that a hint of cinnamon I can smell?"

"Clever girl. Sure is."

"Hey," Jennifer suddenly remembered Toby's words and headed over to the stove, "can I help? Have you been feeling okay?"

Nan's brow wrinkled in confusion. "I'm perfectly fine."

"You are?"

"Last time I checked I was." She chuckled as she flipped another pancake.

"Oh." Jennifer stiffened and looked around. "Where's Toby?"

"Here he is. He went to fetch the paper."

"Good morning, Jen." Toby walked in and gave Nan a noisy kiss.

"Oh, stop it, young man. You should be kissing your beautiful girlfriend, not me."

"Ah... I'm not..."

Jennifer's words were cut short by a light kiss from Toby.

"I hope you weren't about to tell Nan you're not hungry. Nobody ever refuses her pancakes." Toby quirked a brow.

What the heck? Now she had to steady her thumping heart and not let the shock of the kiss show on her face.

"Here you go." Nan passed her the tower of pancakes.

Jennifer managed a stilted smile and placed it on the table. "Thanks, Nan." When Nan turned back to the kitchen sink, Jennifer glared at Toby.

Seemingly unaffected, he took the seat beside her and served a pancake onto her plate.

"What's going on?" she hissed quietly. "Your grandmother doesn't need our help."

"Nan was a famous chocolate maker in her day, Jen. Have I told you before?" Toby spoke to the room at large, including Nan in the conversation when she joined them at the table.

Jennifer's hand tightened around the knife she was using to spread the butter. "No, you must have overlooked it," she ground out.

Toby passed the jam next and gave her one of his smiles. One which usually left her melting. "We're going to help Nan make chocolates for the hospital fete next week."

"Hope you don't mind?" Nan asked.

Toby fleetingly touched her wrist, just as Jennifer roughly swallowed her first bite. She coughed to clear it when the doorbell rang.

"Oh, that must be my cocoa. I've been worried sick it wouldn't arrive in time."

As Nan sped away, Jennifer twisted around to glare at him. "You *lied* to me?"

"No, I didn't."

"Stop it, Toby."

"You would've never agreed to come if I'd told you we were making chocolates."

"Of course not. How important is making chocolates compared to getting a promotion?"

"See what I mean?"

"What do you mean?" she hissed, keeping her voice down.

"Your career is more important."

"I know that."

"And since you're not an authority on grandmothers, I had to use any means I could."

"But your grandmother thinks I'm your girlfriend."

"It makes her happy. Pleasing—"

Nan reappeared with the cocoa. "Well, that's everything we need to get started."

Jennifer zipped her mouth.

"Who's pleasing who?" Nan asked, taking her seat again.

Toby laughed. "I'll try pleasing you both."

❧

"Okay, Nan, what music will it be today?" Toby asked, waving his phone in the air.

Nan had the stove fired up with a large pot of cocoa, butter, milk, and sugar. She looked across with a large smile. "Is this the promised playlist?"

"Sure is, with all your favourites."

Jennifer quirked an eyebrow, just as Bon Jovi's *Living on a Prayer* started blaring from the speakers.

"Here's an apron, dear." Nan searched a nearby drawer one-handed, with the other hand stirring firmly.

Jennifer took the pink, frilly apron, and bit down on her lip, holding back a chuckle.

"How about our first dance, Nan? Jen can take over for a minute."

Nan handed over the spoon. "Stir gently," she instructed.

Jennifer watched in amusement as Toby took Nan by one hand and twirled her around, before adding an Elvis Presley pelvis move. The kitchen wasn't big enough for this kind of dancing and despite her initial annoyance for how Toby got her there, Jennifer laughed along with Nan's giggling.

"Oh, Toby, I'm not as young as I used to be."

"Nan, you're only as old as you feel."

Nan put her hand to her back and took some big breaths. "Dance the next one with Jennifer."

"Ah... no, it's fine, I can't. I'm wearing an apron."

"That excuse doesn't work in this kitchen. Toby will never settle down to work if he doesn't get a dance in with everyone."

Jennifer groaned when Phil Collins' *Against All Odds* came on next. In battered jeans and a chest-hugging navy shirt, Toby made a big show of welcoming her into his arms for the slow dance.

"Great song, don't you think, Nan?" Toby smiled, as the music mellowed his moves.

"I wish I got the slow one. That fast stuff is too much for this old body."

Toby chuckled and Jennifer danced with a stiff back. "Relax, Jen, it's only one dance and it makes Nan happy to see us enjoying ourselves," Toby whispered near her ear, which only succeeded in setting every pulse alive in her body. She pushed back a fraction and looked up. She swayed momentarily at the tender look that replaced his smile. Timidly resting her face against his chest, she swallowed, warmed by the quiet thud of his beating heart against her cheek.

After the dancing, the serious task of chocolate making began. The music continued in the background with barely a song that Toby didn't know the words to. This was a new side to Toby she never imagined. He unashamedly joked his way through the day and embedded himself further into her heart with every smile he turned her way. His adorable interaction with his grandmother touched a raw spot when she watched them together. She feared she would not come away from this weekend unscathed.

෯෬෯

It was early afternoon before Jennifer thought to ask, "So, tell me, why are your chocolates so famous, Nan?"

"It's the special flavours she puts in," Toby answered for her.

"I try to keep it secret, but since you're the first girl Toby has brought here, I'll let you in on a few," Nan said coyly.

Jennifer quirked a brow in Toby's direction only to get a shrug in response. "Are you sure there hasn't been even one, Nan?"

"I'm sure. He's only ever talked about one girl and if you're the short, beautiful one he works with, then it can only be you."

Jennifer rolled her eyes at the short reference. When she looked across at Toby, there were no funny comebacks, no jokes, just the same look she'd witnessed when they danced.

The flutter in her heart amplified, and with shaking hands, Jennifer got back to removing the hardened chocolates from the moulds and setting the flower petals on top.

"It's my interesting flavour combinations—"

Jennifer didn't need to hear them. The mixture of aromas swirling around her head all day still lingered in the air. There was the hint of apple and cinnamon — her favourite. The infusion of different fruits and berries, strawberries and chopped up lemons and limes. Mixed with the mouth-watering aroma of melted chocolate, the flavours had left her stomach begging for chocolate all day. Tomorrow's batch would concentrate on herbs, spices and garlic. How those flavours combined with chocolate she wasn't so sure, but she could hardly wait.

By the end of the day, Jennifer knew she'd found a kindred spirit. She could relate to the hardworking and dedicated grandmother. This project was no mean feat, and tomorrow they would do it all again.

"Okay, time for a break." Toby rose and stretched, before cranking up the music.

"No dancing for me, please," Nan begged, "my back's killing me."

Toby picked up a sauce bottle and sang along with Robert

Palmer's, *Bad Case of Loving You*. Nan joined in for a verse while Jennifer enjoyed a good laugh. Everything about this day intensified her feelings.

Before the song ended, Toby reached over and gave her a lingering kiss. "Thanks for coming."

All the air whooshed out of her lungs and her laughter stopped dead in its tracks.

"Here you go, Toby," Nan said, holding up a chocolate. "This is the heart I promised to make for you when you met the perfect girl."

Jennifer spluttered and managed to breathe again.

Toby killed the music and frowned. "Nan, what are you talking about?"

"Well, let me see. You might have been about eight years old." She chuckled, then gave Jennifer a wink. "I'll leave you pair for a bit. This nanna needs a short nap."

CRRD

Jennifer fiddled with the handle of her mug, as she settled on the back patio.

Toby absently stirred his drink. He'd gone awkwardly quiet after Nan's announcement. "I'm sorry about Nan, just then."

Jennifer swallowed a mouthful as Toby's gaze drew level with hers. "Don't be. She's great. I wish I was close to a grandmother."

Toby grimaced. "Yeah, she's been the best all my life, but she *never* holds back."

Jennifer chuckled, but tore her gaze away and looked out into Nan's garden. When Toby's chair squeaked, she turned back. Toby had risen, a vulnerable look on his face.

"Is our break over?" she asked, the hot tea swirling in her stomach.

His hands curled by his side. "No, no, sorry, finish your drink. I'll be back in a minute."

She took a deep breath when he walked away. No doubt he would tell her in his own time what was unsettling him. Turning back to the garden, she exhaled and allowed her shoulders to relax. Roses of all colours fought for her attention just as a Ulysses butterfly flitted past her vision. The heady fragrances drifted on the light afternoon breeze and tantalised her senses. A family of curlews on their long, spindly legs nervously walked across the back yard, adding to the postcard view.

A sudden thick wad of emotion built up inside her chest. This was so idyllic compared to the rushed lifestyle she lived every day. She lived and worked in high-rises and went weeks without seeing a single blade of grass. Was this weekend a wake-up call? Was her career really that important?

She started when Toby returned and pushed his chair in.

"Jen, this was always meant for you."

Huh? Toby placed the chocolate heart Nan had made earlier onto her palm. Iced on top were the words, 'You and Me'.

Her breath caught in her throat.

"I always wanted to give 'us' a go, but I've never known how to ask."

"Ask what?" She wouldn't dare let her heart go there.

Toby groaned and ploughed a hand through his hair. "I like you a lot, Jen."

Jennifer focused on the chocolate heart. When its edges blurred, she blinked furiously and breathed in deeply. "Well," she chided, "that took you long enough."

"What?"

It took a few moments for the confused expression to leave his face. When his mouth turned up at its edges, she knew he'd finally worked it out.

"Really?"

Jennifer nodded and smiled with relief.

Toby leaned closer until their foreheads touched and chuckled. "Wow, I'll have to thank Nan for the chocolate heart. It was the push I needed."

"Can we visit her more often?"

Toby sat back a fraction and captured her face. "Yeah, I guess we can."

"Because I like her a lot."

"Me too, but let's hope we can get her to bed early to practise our presentation."

Jennifer sank into his touch, enjoying the way her heart blossomed. "I'm not so sure if the promotion is as important anymore."

Toby quirked an eyebrow. "All because of a chocolate heart and a garden full of roses?"

Jennifer tapped her mouth with her finger, thinking hard. Then she pointed towards a bright cluster of roses she'd noticed earlier. "I'll have a red one please."

A huge smile lit up Toby's face. "I don't think Nan will mind, but first, can I do this?"

Jennifer was unprepared for the kiss that sent tingles along her skin. It filled her with an essence of roses, chocolates, and grandmothers, and left her wanting more.

She'd have to thank Nan for the chocolate heart too.

6

HOT CHOCOLATE AND HEAVEN

CAROLINE DENESS

August 1816

M ajor Will Fraser reached up to lift Mrs Caitlyn Halliday down from her streaming horse. A sudden downpour, as they explored his brother's estate, left the pair separated from the rest of the party.

Slipping a little in a puddle, Will overbalanced and Cait slid onto his chest, leaving heat down his front as she slid to the ground. He steadied Cait on the ground, then touched his lips to her forehead, noting her sharp intake of breath, and her small hands pushing his chest as she stumbled back.

"What are you doing, Major?" Cait's grey eyes stormed, and the delicate skin of her cheeks flamed.

"I – I'm – forgive me, Cait. I slipped." What *could* he say? He'd dreamed of her in his arms for months.

He took the horses' bridles and led them to shelter.

CЖ❧

Thoughts of Cait had possessed Will since he had returned her husband's effects the previous year. Her light hair, pale translucent skin, and haunted eyes.

Captain Halliday had lost his life in the final charge at Waterloo. Such a mindless waste, as they had pushed their exhausted horses over the dead, dying and screaming souls covering that blood splattered plain.

Will could still see her face crumple as she looked at the bag he held. Knowing all he was returning to her were painful memories.

He had wanted to take her in his arms then, but honour forbade it.

The atmosphere lightened when a high-pitched voice approached. "Mama, Mama, who is it?" The little boy threw his arms around her legs and looked up, fixing his soulful gaze on Will. "Who are you?"

"Major William Fraser, at your service, young man. A friend of your father. Now, you must be Thomas, if I'm not mistaken?"

Mrs Cait Halliday had looked on, apparently stunned, as Will had shaken the young boy's hand.

CЖ❧

Brought back to the present by the thundering rain on the roof, Will held his hand out to lead Cait inside.

"I'll get a fire going in the lodge for you to warm up."

The fire was already set, and it caught easily as Will struck the flint. Cait had looked angry as she waited for him to open the door, her glare could have cut ice.

How could he lighten the atmosphere?

How did he lay his heart at her feet, without being trampled?

"Come and warm yourself, my dear. I'll search out a towel for your wet hair."

CRBO

Automatically following the major into the lodge, Cait realised she was shivering as she stood in front of the window. The heat that spread through her body, when she came into contact with the major's chest, had dissipated. She moved to stand by the crackling blaze.

Her galloping pulse was another matter. Angry at herself, as much as the major, Cait willed her heart rate to slow.

How did his touch affect her like this?

It was over twelve months since Mark had been killed. Despite putting off her mourning clothes, Cait still felt weighed down by grief and regret. And worry for Thomas.

She had loved Mark, but it had been a safe, calm affection: reassuring. The major left her feeling caught in a whirlpool – out of her depth and dizzy. Why *did* this man affect her senses so?

A tingle of awareness slid down her back. She shivered.

"Here, Cait, dry yourself with these."

Cait took a deep breath. Turning, she looked up at the tanned, squared jaw, the battle-hardened face, framed by dark hair, softened only by laughter lines radiating from his treacle eyes when he smiled.

"I don't remember asking you to call me Cait, Major." She attempted to look stern, trying to depress his presumption.

∞

Drawn to the luminous skin, Will was almost caught staring at the vulnerable curve of Cait's neck. His lips wanted to taste her warmth. Then she shivered and he remembered the towels in his hands.

Now she looked gloriously annoyed.

"I'm sorry, Mrs Halliday, but Mark always called you Cait, and I seem to have caught the habit. Forgive me?"

Kicking himself for reminding her of Mark, Will watched her face go still. The last thing he wanted was to upset her. Her eyes sheened with tears. Then she blinked.

"No need. I'm sorry to quibble. You've been very kind. It must be the weather upsetting me. I don't like to leave Thomas with strangers for too long. Please, call me Cait."

Grateful, he accepted the peace offering. "Thank you, Cait. Dry yourself, and I'll explore the cupboards for supplies."

Leaving Cait to warm up, Will went to see what treasures he could unearth. The lodge was usually kept stocked with necessities for situations such as this. It looked as though cook had sent over something today: a cloth covered pile sat in the middle of the small dining table.

"Success, Cook must have divined the weather. We have bread, butter, and cheese, and even a jug of milk. I hope there is still some cocoa in the cupboard. My brother always loved it as a lad."

Will smiled across at the woman who inhabited his dreams.

He had called on her as regularly as possible in the last year, and occasionally saw her in the local village. He and Mark had been friends as boys. They had met up again just prior to Waterloo, when Will found Mark in charge of one of his two companies of cavalry men.

The moment Will saw Cait, he had felt protective towards her, and her young son.

CR8D

As he uttered the word 'cocoa', Cait was on her feet, and beside Will at the cupboard.

"Is there a pan to heat the milk for cocoa?"

Will hid a grin.

So chocolate was the way to this woman's heart?

Looking down at the strawberry blond curls springing out from the edges of her hair as it dried, he smiled. He found a pan, Cait poured in the milk and then stirred in the cocoa, before Will hung the pot over the fire. Cait then positioned herself by the fire, with a spoon for stirring.

"This is Thomas's favourite as well."

Will grinned as Cait looked up.

"They probably still serve warm cocoa for afternoon tea in the nursery."

"In that case, Thomas won't miss me for a while."

"I hope not. I like having you all to myself. I'd like to spend more time with you, Cait."

Will felt relieved to have finally dragged up the courage to say even that much. He didn't want to rush Cait, hence he'd waited more than a year to say anything. But still, it felt a bit like approaching an enemy stronghold. Heart pounding and hoping for the best, while preparing for the worst.

"And Thomas, too. He's a brave little scamp." Will didn't want Cait to feel he would leave her son out, and he certainly didn't want her to think him jealous of Mark's legacy.

Mark had asked him to look after the pair if anything went wrong in the battle that day. Mark had worried that Cait's spendthrift brother would encroach. In fact, Mark admitted the main reason he had married Cait was to protect her. Her father was ailing, and he knew her brother was not to be trusted.

∽∾

"Major," Cait began, as she bent to stir the cocoa. Looking up, she found him observing her with a lop-sided grin. Her heart did a curious thump in her chest before speeding up. It was such a wistful expression on his face, tinged with longing.

"Please, call me William. I have sold out, after all."

Cait sighed. Still not quite sure what to say, or how she felt. "William, then. I'm not sure what you mean? What you want? It feels so strange being here with you." *I don't understand what is happening to me.*

"Strange, good, or strange, bad?" The major grinned at her.

"There you go again, asking questions I can't answer." Cait bit her lip, trying to hide a grin at his annoying questions. Could the fluttery feeling inside her be good?

William obviously caught her grin and decided to press on.

"While I didn't engineer the rain, I hope it will last a bit longer. Is there any chance you could see your way to relaxing in my company, even enjoying it, as I do yours?"

"Why do you...?" Cait leapt for the pot, grasping the handle with a towel. "It's ready." She laughed. "Our chocolate."

Cait sighed with relief as William poured the cocoa into mugs. Realising she actually liked his company. He had a reassuring presence, but she didn't like the flustered feelings when he looked at her. A feeling she didn't recognise.

Sitting at the table, both hands wrapped around the warm mug, Cait inhaled the familiar scent: her comfort food as a child. "Mmm, that smells so good." Then she sipped. "Ah, heaven."

Cait looked over as William's mouth quirked up at one end, and suddenly she didn't feel quite as alone as she had since losing Mark. Strengthened by the possibility that she might have a choice, other than succumbing to her brother's more and more forceful persuasions to marry his business partner. She exhaled with relief.

⋘⋙

Will watched, fascinated, and barely suppressed a groan as her pale pink lips sipped the cocoa. If only Cait appreciated him as much, he would be in heaven too. She looked up, and he felt trapped in her uncertain gaze; hoping his longing was not overwhelming. He grinned, trying to relax, and took a sip of his own cocoa.

"Ah, even better than when my brother and I were young."

"William, why did your brother and his wife ask Thomas and me to this house party? I hardly know them."

"Because you deserve some amusement. And because I asked them to include you. Now, what else can I do to—?" His words were cut off by a peremptory knocking at the door. "I knew this was too good to last," he muttered.

ᏨᎢᏨᎦ

Will strode to the door, wondering why anyone would be looking for them so soon.

"Where's Cait?" the man at the door demanded, stumbling past Will, and into the room. Will caught a strong whiff of brandy from the younger man.

"Good god, David, what are you doing here? I hope Lord and Lady Fraser didn't see you like this?"

Will watched as Cait approached – her brother – presumably.

"You were s'posed to be home to meet my partner, Cait."

"David, I've told you I won't marry him. I said I wouldn't be there."

Then David made the mistake of grabbing Cait's shoulders and shaking her. "Why not?" he whined.

Will pulled the sulky interloper back from Cait with one arm around his upper chest and used the other to twist David's arm behind his back.

"That's not how you treat a lady." Will stated. "Apologise."

"She's my sister."

"All the more reason to look after her." Will twisted the idiot's arm a bit more to emphasise his point.

"Thank you, Major." Will saw Cait's smile dawn.

"My pleasure, Mrs Halliday. This is your brother, I presume. What do you want me to do with him?"

Cait laughed, obviously considering the possibilities.

"Tell him to let me go, Cait." David looked as though he was attempting an ingratiating smile, but the result was more grimace. "Tell him I'm harmless."

"If the major lets you go, do you promise to forget about me marrying your partner?"

"But Cait, he loves you. And he'll increase my share of the club if you do."

"Have you no insight, David? He sees me as an asset. Or are you so in debt to him, you'll do whatever he asks?"

Will felt David tense as Cait asked about debt. They were getting to the basis of the problem it seemed. Cait looked disgusted.

"How can you keep gambling away the estate our father built so carefully? You're no longer a child, David Melling. You need to take responsibility, and I will not be pulled down into the mire with you. I have Thomas to look after. You're his uncle. You should be helping me."

Will saw the disappointed look on Cait's face before she turned to pace the room.

"Well, Melling, seems you have been given your marching orders. Time to explain the situation to your partner and leave your sister alone." Will let go of the drooping man and escorted him to the door.

Before Will closed the door, however, Welling turned back. "Don't you care for the estate, Cait? It'll be your fault if I have to sell the land."

"No, David, you refused my help with managing the land. The blame rests squarely with your greed and abysmal head for cards." She turned and headed back to the fire, obviously agitated by her brother's threat.

"You'll regret this, Cait," David yelled, before he slouched off.

Closing the door, the major walked over to stand behind Cait. After a moment he put his hands, gently, on her shoulders. "Is there anything I can do to help, Cait? Another cup of hot chocolate? You don't have to deal with him by yourself."

Cait's shoulders slumped. The major's hands were so comforting. His words as soothing as the warm cocoa he offered. No-one had ever stood up for her against her older brother before. Mark would have done it, but he hadn't been there.

It was all too much. Cait turned and buried her face in his shoulder, struggling to hold back tears. When his arms encircled her, she couldn't. His embrace tightened as she sobbed.

"I don't know what to do about David. I'm sure his partner is bleeding him dry to get whatever is not entailed on the estate. But David just won't see it." She sniffed.

"Come," William said, holding her shoulders, as he stepped back to see Cait's assuredly, woebegone face. He handed her his handkerchief. "Let's sit down and discuss this. Perhaps I can get my brother to look into this partner's background. Is the estate profitable?"

Cait sat. William's calm approach helped her think logically. She dried her eyes. "The estate definitely *was* profitable. I was helping Father run it during his illness. So I could certainly help David. He was never at home to learn what was needed. But since my father's death two years ago, David and his so-called partner, have taken over. Even though Father appointed our solicitor as joint trustee until David turns thirty. Luckily, there are some funds David can't get at.

"I'm sorry, William, I shouldn't be involving you in any of this. You're too easy to confide in. I blame the cocoa." She tried to joke, producing a wan smile.

"Cait, there is nothing I would like better than to help you in this. To shoulder these burdens with you."

ೞೞ

Will couldn't wait any longer. He had to tell her how he felt and hope she didn't run for the hills.

He took her hands.

"Cait, I love you. I want you to be my wife. I know it's soon after Mark's death, but there is nothing I would like more than to spend the rest of my life with you and Thomas by my side. I would be proud to be his stepfather." Will hoped Cait could see the love in his eyes. And not be overwhelmed by the desire he was trying to control. He felt her hands flutter at his declaration of love.

ೞೞ

Cait felt heat spread over her face as she looked at William's capable hands over her own. She felt a mixture of reassurance and panic at his words. Wanting help from someone, needing love, but somehow feeling caught on a runaway horse – out of control. Raising her eyes to his face, she found such a tender expression on it, she stopped breathing.

"Cait, please, let me help. I can have our man of business look into things through your solicitor. Especially if we're discussing marriage settlements." He smiled and released her hands.

Cait tensed, she didn't want to be manoeuvred into a hasty marriage, but she did feel stronger with William beside her. Were these fluttery feelings *more* than attraction? His smile did such odd things to her insides.

"Sweetheart, I don't want to push you." It was as though he read her mind. "You can draw back at any time if you don't feel comfortable. But it would be a more legitimate way to assess the problem. We don't have to make a public announcement until you are satisfied."

Gradually Cait's arms relaxed, her knuckles losing their whiteness. William went down on one knee before her and gently took her hands again.

"Cait, my love, would you please do me the honour of becoming my wife?" He looked into the depths of her eyes, and grinned. "Or, at least, consider it?"

It was William's smile that did it. Its warmth spread through Cait like hot chocolate and gave her the courage to grasp a second chance at happiness.

"Yes," Cait said. "Yes, I'll consider it."

With a whoop, Will stood, pulling her into his arms. He tipped up her chin for a kiss – a speaking kiss – a kiss he hoped told Cait how much he loved and needed her.

He felt Cait flutter in his arms before sinking against him, gripping his lapels and sighing as she opened to him and dived into passion. She was obviously giving this serious consideration and he couldn't be happier. Maybe, one of these days, she might even compare *him* to heaven?

7
CHOCOLATE AND ORANGE

LOUISA DUVAL

Vicki

I glanced out the window of the mini-bus and saw a sign at the front of the Ballydoon Christmas Markets: *Kissing Booth with Hot Santa. Photos $10. Proceeds to the Rural Fire Brigade.*

"Kissing booth?" I muttered, screwing up my nose. "I can't believe it. In this day and age."

"Stop clutching your pearls, Vicki. Have some fun." Resident troublemaker of the aged care home, Beryl, appeared at my side with four others. "Santa photo, everyone. Like last year. And I want a firefighter calendar, too."

At least outings with Beryl and her cronies were never dull.

I helped the last of the aged care residents off the bus and approached the Hot Santa stall. Swathes of long, thin, yellow-green leaves were tied with red ribbon to the stall's shade cover, gently rustling in the breeze.

"Native mistletoe." Beryl pointed to a sprig of the same leaves suspended over a red chaise for the photos.

The mistletoe garlands connected the photo booth to the stall next door. I paused, seeing the sign: 'Heavenly Chocolate'. I immediately remembered high school; the aches and sweat of hockey training every Tuesday followed by talking at my locker with Josh Cavanagh, who made me laugh and always had chocolates from his mother's shop.

My eyes strayed to a pile of Josh Cavanagh's cookbooks, *Sweet Treats*. The boy I'd known was now a celebrity chef. His smile on the cover was the perfect balance between sweet and sin. My stomach fluttered. I averted my gaze, finding myself staring at calendars of half-dressed, local firefighters.

"Kisses strictly on the cheek? You've got to be kidding me." Beryl scowled at the photographer. "Hey, Sammie, I'll give Hot Santa twenty bucks if he kisses me on the lips."

The photographer laughed as I strode over to Beryl, hands on hips.

"Beryl, take it down a notch."

"Party pooper." At eighty-three, she was as cunning as she was cheeky. "Vicki, you need a kiss from Hot Santa to get the knot out of your knickers."

Been a while since anyone had been in my knickers.

"Wait – Vicki Jones?" the photographer asked.

I met the photographer's eyes. "Oh, my god, Samantha Jennings?"

She grinned. "Yep. I haven't seen you since high school."

"Yeah, nine years. I'm back home now, finishing my nursing degree online."

"Welcome back." Sam paused, and then nodded to the chocolate stall. "Josh's back, too. Bought his mum's chocolate shop."

"Like, back for good?" I gulped. *Why was I gulping?* Nine years was ancient history for a little high school crush.

Sam nodded.

I cleared my throat. "Mum said she saw him in town."

"You were off to the Olympics for hockey when we graduated." Sam adjusted the camera tripod. "How'd ya go?"

My smile faded. My leg ached on cue. At least Josh had followed his dream: opened a fancy restaurant, been on TV, released a cookbook, and had legions of fans on social media, including me.

Beryl interrupted before I had to answer.

"Hot damn, I'd pay fifty if he'd let me sit on his lap."

Her eyes had lit up at something over my shoulder.

I turned, and saw Hot Santa: shirtless, in red pants and black combat-style boots with a fake snow-white beard and matching wig with red beanie.

Santa did *not* have a belly that wobbled like jelly. His six-pack glistened with sweat. We all watched spellbound as he poured water on a facecloth, his forearms flexing, and then wiped his chest, shoulders and lastly, his arms.

My jaw dropped.

"You're catching flies, sweetie," Beryl winked. I slammed my mouth shut and swatted at an actual fly buzzing around my nose.

Beryl sauntered off to Sam, waving several notes. "Hook me up, Sammie."

"Alright, take your seat with Hot Santa," Sam said, taking Beryl's cash.

Hot Santa sat in the middle of the red chaise. Beryl whooped. "I've got his lap!"

Before I could intervene, she threw her arms around his neck, whispering something in his ear as the others sat around them for the photo.

Sam bent down behind the camera. "Say 'Hot Santa'."

Everyone did, except Hot Santa, as the camera clicked several times. "Come and choose which one you want printed, guys."

⊶⊷

Josh

"My kisses are melting!"

"The kissing booth that good?" Mum chuckled.

"You know I mean our chocolate truffle kisses. It's too damn hot," I hissed back, then chugged down the rest of my water.

The spike in Christmas orders was insane. Everyone wanted Heavenly Chocolate's truffles this year. Selling chocolates in Santa beard, wig and pants in this heat saying "Ho, ho, ho!" for the camera in between customers had turned me into the Grinch.

"Calm your farm, Joshua. I'll be there in fifteen with cold packs and eskies after I drop off an order for Maggie Jones." She paused. "You remember her daughter, Vicki, from high school?"

My stomach somersaulted. "Of course."

"Maggie said Vicki is back in town."

"Okay."

"She's single, too," Mum added too casually.

I spluttered my water. "Right."

Mum chuckled again and hung up.

I grimaced. Mum knew exactly how much I'd liked Vicki Jones during high school. I sighed and helped myself to a truffle.

Still magnificent but too soft from the heat.

Sam appeared with more firefighter calendars for the stall.

"It's really good you bought your mum's shop and are back," she said, pinching a truffle. "And thanks for doing the photo booth. We're making a killing today."

My inner Grinch wavered as Sam smiled at the calendar's cover featuring her best friend, Stacey, who'd almost died from severe burns in a bushfire ten years ago.

"Glad I could help. Got my first controlled burn with the brigade next weekend."

"Bet you didn't count on firefighting when you became a chef."

I snorted. "It was the Santa suit that I didn't see coming."

The Hot Santa kissing booth was Sam's idea: $10 for a photo and a peck on the cheek.

At least no one recognised me under this ridiculous wig and beard.

"Heads up," Sam murmured. "It's the oldies again."

I ducked behind the stall's screen to grab a drink as a minibus pulled up from the aged care home. I almost dropped my bottled water as out from it emerged Vicki Jones.

I hadn't seen her since the last day of high school nine years ago.

Two days after graduation, I started a job in the commercial kitchens of a five-star hotel in Brisbane to complete my chef's apprenticeship and had never looked back.

My restaurant had been *the* place to dine at The Rocks in Sydney. I'd had a cooking segment on TV and launched a successful cookbook.

But one look at Vicki and I was a nervous, tongue-tied seventeen-year-old again.

Vicki looked good. *Really* good, if not a little harassed trying to herd five aged care residents through the crowd. Her work uniform — a polo shirt and black shorts that stopped above her knees — didn't hide any of her curves.

Why was a world championship hockey player on a day trip with aged care residents?

Who all eyed me with big grins. *Yikes.* One licked her lips, holding a fistful of cash. Vicki hadn't seen me yet.

I quickly grabbed a washcloth to clean up. I soaked it with water and wiped down my chest, arms and shoulders, feeling instantly cooler. Turning back, I found Vicki openly checking me out, her eyes glazed with desire as she looked me up and down.

Adrenalin pulsed through me.

Move over, Grinch. Hot Santa is here.

I took my seat on the chaise lounge and the woman called Beryl demanded to sit on my lap.

"I'm definitely on your naughty list, Hot Santa," she whispered, clutching my neck.

Oh boy.

They all chorused "Hot Santa" for the camera. I helped Beryl to her feet.

"Vicki, you're up next!" Sam hollered.

I froze.

"What? I'm not..." Vicki gulped. "I haven't paid."

"They did." Sam pointed at Beryl and her mates. "It's their shout."

Beryl cackled while the others grinned. "Come on, Vicki. Support the rural firefighters."

She relented with a sigh.

We'd never touched each other before, save being crammed in a bus seat together. We'd never even held hands. I took my seat again, my palms sweaty; sweatier than they'd been all afternoon in the heat.

"Sit on his lap!" Beryl hooted. Everyone cheered.

"It's okay," I grunted.

Vicki walked up to the chaise. *Did she have a limp?*

"Do you mind if I use your shoulder?"

I shook my head as my fake beard and wig flew around my face in the hot wind.

Vicki held on as she lowered herself to perch on my leg. She wobbled and I grabbed her before she fell; my hand clasping her thigh as her arms wrapped around me.

Goosebumps erupted all over my skin. My heart pounded like I'd just sprinted a race.

"I've got you," I murmured.

I could have sworn her leg had given out on her.

"You okay?"

She nodded, blushing as she met my gaze. *Did she recognise me?*

Vicki blinked, then looked away to the camera.

I inhaled deeply. *Citrus. She smelled like oranges, just like back in high school.* Vicki had always eaten oranges after hockey practice every Tuesday before we caught the late bus.

"Okay, Vicki…" Sam said, holding up one finger. "On the count of three."

I should have asked her out back then.

"One…"

Just ask her if she'd like to get a coffee sometime.

"Two…"

I should reintroduce myself, then ask her for a drink.

"Hey, Vicki—"

I twisted towards her just as she waved her hand suddenly, causing her to lean into me. I instinctively grabbed her thigh again, thinking she was about to fall, and found her lips pressed up against mine.

"Three." The camera's shutter clicked in rapid succession.

Vicki's eyes widened. I held still. Every nerve in my body felt like it had been zapped.

She broke the kiss just as quickly as it had started but didn't move away. My fingers twitched against the soft skin behind her knee. *So damn soft.*

"You taste like chocolate," Vicki breathed.

I couldn't tear my eyes from hers. Couldn't speak. I just stared mutely back.

The aged care residents were cheering "Vicki kissed Hot Santa" at the top of their raspy, asthmatic voices. Sam called out. "Yo, Santa. You can let Vicki go now."

"I-I was s-swatting a fly," Vicki stammered. Her cheeks were as red as my Santa pants. "I'm so sorry. That was totally an accident. I would *never*—"

She slapped a hand over her mouth.

I quickly helped her stand. Vicki stumbled but waved me off.

"Photos will be done in twenty, Vicki." Sam smirked, with one eyebrow arched. "I'll keep your calendars with your photos, too."

"Yeah, sure. Thank you. Great," Vicki mumbled, moving away.

"Wait!" I wrestled with the beanie, wig and beard, the elastic getting caught on my ears. When I'd finally escaped the Santa disguise, Vicki had disappeared into the crowd with five of the fastest octogenarians in existence.

"Customers, Chef Santa." Sam said, pointing to my chocolate stall. "I'll set up for the next photo."

An idea struck me so hard I faltered. Something I'd never tried and yet the flavours had always been right in front of me.

"Can you do me a favour, Sam? Please. Mind the stall. I'll be right back. I promise."

CRT80

Vicki

An hour later, the aged care residents waited in the comfort of the mini-bus's air-conditioning as I collected our photos and calendars.

No one was at the chocolate stall. Half of the stock was already packed in eskies. All I could think about were chocolate truffles since that kiss.

Please have some truffles left. Mum had texted at the last minute, asking me to buy some truffles at the markets.

Sam was also gone, and mercifully, the photo booth. And no Hot Santa. I sighed – with relief or regret, I wasn't sure.

"Um, hello?" I called out.

Something, or someone, shuffled under the table.

A head popped up and said, "Hang on a sec – Vicki Jones!"

"Oh, Josh." I giggled like a schoolgirl with a crush, as he stood, wearing a polo with the chocolate shop logo. "I haven't seen you since—"

"Last day of high school cleaning out our lockers." His cheeks were flushed.

He must be hot.

My cheeks burst into flame. "I'm surprised you remember me."

"Are you kidding?" he said. "I'd never forget the badass hockey player, school locker neighbour and late bus friend on Tuesdays."

"Oh." Butterflies took flight in my stomach.

He wiped his palms on – *red pants.*

Red. Santa. Pants.

My hand flew to my mouth, remembering the kiss. His eyes flicked down to my lips. That wasn't just a look: he smouldered.

I pointed at his pants. "You're Hot Santa!"

Josh's face paled.

A horn honked.

"Hurry up, Vicki," Beryl called from the bus. "I don't want to miss dinner. It's trifle night."

I looked away, blinking as I recognised a face on the firefighting calendars.

"Wait, you're Mr July, too?" I squeaked.

"Yeah, I was Christmas in July." He cringed. "Hence, the Hot Santa costume for the photo booth."

My mind reeled. I'd kissed Hot Santa who was also my high school crush, by accident, having had no idea it was him.

"You were going to try out for the Olympic hockey team," he said in a rush. "I looked up the Aussie team, but I never saw your name."

The exhilaration of kissing him plummeted. Pain twinged in my leg, and I winced.

"Are you okay? I noticed you were limping before."

"Nasty accident at the selection trials. I broke my femur and fractured my hip. Two rounds of surgery, four pins in the bone. Sometimes it flares up." I bit my lip. "No Olympics. No more hockey."

CRXO

Josh

"I'm so sorry—"

"Don't be." Vicki's chin wobbled. She sucked in a breath and pasted on a false smile. "Thought I'd work in coaching but..." Her smile became softer, genuine. "I met some awesome nurses during my recovery, and I decided to enrol in a nursing degree. I'm back home while I finish my studies online. Going to do my prac at the hospital."

She jerked her thumb at the mini-bus. "I work at the aged care home."

I grinned, not wanting to point out the obvious about her uniform. In high school, she'd talked so passionately about wanting to make the Olympic hockey team. The fire in her eyes as she talked about nursing was the same as the Vicki I'd known years ago: all grit and determination.

"You'll be a badass and awesome nurse, Vicki."

My eyes strayed to her lips again. *Our kiss.*

"Sorry about..." I coughed. "What happened before."

"You're apologising to me?"

Vicki's smile curled into something flirty.

And I liked it. A lot.

"I'm sorry you had to sit on me. I was a sweaty mess today." *Real smooth, Josh.*

"God, I'm pretty sure I stank every Tuesday after hockey training."

"You smelled like oranges." My voice dropped an octave lower. "You always did. Still do."

She met my gaze. I didn't hide any of my hunger for her.

"You tasted like chocolate," she breathed. "You always had chocolates from your mum's shop on Tuesdays."

"Because the pretty, sporty girl on the bus always liked them."

Vicki smiled – a broad, mega-watt smile. I felt like a king.

The bus horn honked again, ruining the moment.

"I should get our calendars and photos," Vicki said. "And go."

"Right. Yes."

I found a bag with their purchases that Sam had left for Vicki.

"Should all be in there." I handed it over, our hands brushing.

Fire roared up my arm.

Yet again, I'd become mute.

"Right, thank you." Vicki clutched the bag. "I should go." But she didn't move.

Come on, Josh. Speak!

"Well, it was good to see you, Josh."

She spun on her heel and headed for the bus.

"Wait!"

I moved around the stall's table and stopped before her.

"I owe you another apology."

Vicki slowly turned around, frowning.

"I'm sorry I never asked you out in high school. And I'm sorry about the kiss. Not that we did kiss. That was great. I mean, I'm sorry our first kiss happened that way. That's not how I would have planned to kiss you. If that's what you wanted me to do."

Everything came down to this moment. Did she want me, or Hot Santa?

Vicki suddenly lunged, her bag of photos crashing to the ground. She fisted my collar, pulling me close, and kissed me without hesitation.

I groaned, cupped her face, and savoured her: Vicki, the girl of my dreams. Kissing her was better than chocolate: this kiss was the perfect blend of sweetness and sin. Better than any fantasy or dream I'd had about what kissing her would be like.

We pulled apart to the sound of clapping, both of us breathing hard. The aged care residents were giving us a standing ovation on the mini-bus.

I couldn't stop smiling. "I have something for you. A new truffle. Would you like to try it?"

Vicki nodded, and I pulled out a box from an esky.

"It's an experiment with a traditional chocolate truffle." I swallowed hard. "I bought a locally made orange liqueur today, mixed it with the truffles and reshaped them, and dusted them with dark cocoa."

"Chocolate and orange?" she whispered, picking one up.

"Inspired by a kiss."

Vicki took a bite and moaned, then popped the rest into her mouth.

"Well?" This was the most stressful wait for a review of one of my recipes I'd ever had. "Is it okay?"

"Perfect combination," Vicki whispered.

My chest swelled. "Are you free Boxing Day? In the afternoon?"

"That's Tuesday," Vicki grinned. "I'm free. And Josh? Bring chocolates."

8

HOT LIKE CHOCOLATE

AMY HUTTON

Mud splattered the front of her boots as she tramped through the wet slush. Whoever said New York was beautiful when it snowed, failed to mention what it was like when the magical blanket of white melted. It was slippery and grimy, with brown sludge piled along the footpaths, and filthy, freezing puddles lay in wait to shower unsuspecting pedestrians.

Gina moved to New York two years earlier, leaving her life in Sydney behind to follow her dreams. The only time she regretted that decision was when the streets became dirt covered ice-rinks, or when the weather turned so humid the subways smelled like armpits.

Her feet skidded beneath her, and she quickly grabbed a 'No Stopping' sign to steady herself.

"Today of all days," she muttered, as she ducked the spray from a passing cyclist.

Today she wanted to appear her absolute best. Happy, successful, glamorous, together. One hundred percent New York.

Instead, she was dishevelled and grotty, her flame red hair frizzy from the light sleet, and her expensive new jeans dotted with splodges of dirt.

And now she was running late, which meant she wouldn't have time to fix herself up before she saw him. Him being Greg. Her ex-first love, Greg. He was in town to promote his new cookbook, *Hot Like Chocolate*, and she was the producer assigned to his segment on KNBC's *Big Apple Talk*, New York's top-rating daytime chat show.

"You're late," Tessa barked as Gina slid breathlessly into a seat and joined the morning meeting.

Gina pushed her soggy fringe out of her eyes and smiled at her boss. "Sorry. The snow."

Tessa gave a dismissive eye roll. "We're discussing your friend, Greg James. How well do you know him?"

Gina shuffled in her chair. "We kind of grew up together."

"Oh, really? Tell us everything," Tessa said, with an emphasis on 'everything'.

Gina scrambled to decide what to say. Should she tell them about the blueness of his eyes, or how his black hair shimmers like glittering coal as it flops around his face. Or how pillowy soft his lips are, and how wide they spread over his perfect teeth when he smiles. Or should she mention that when he kisses, he likes to gently bite your bottom lip.

"I haven't seen him for about six years," she finally settled on. "We met when I was fourteen and he was sixteen. But I haven't really seen him since he left to work in his uncle's restaurant in Melbourne."

"What about before he left," Tessa said. "You must have some fun stories."

Well, there was this one time my friend's mum busted us in the back of Greg's van, with his hands up my top, Gina thought, though she doubted getting felt up over her bra was something she wanted discussed on television.

"One time he nearly burnt down his parents' kitchen when he forgot he had a chocolate cake in the oven. Is that the kind of thing?" Gina didn't mention he forgot because he was too busy kissing her.

"Perfect. That's exactly the kind of thing. Unless you have anything more..." Tessa paused for effect, her immaculate eyebrows raised suggestively. "Personal?"

Gina shook her head. "Not that I remember off hand," she lied.

Tessa shrugged. "Well, it's your segment. Come up with something fun." She made a shooing motion.

Gina nodded and gathered her things. "Fun personal stories. Right," she said as she tried to think of something fun that didn't involve Greg's tongue in her mouth.

"And don't forget to ask about Sadie," Tessa bellowed after her.

Gina's shoulders drooped. Sadie was the Aussie supermodel Greg was dating.

☚☞

When Gina first met Greg, it had been love at first sight. At least it was for her.

He was a couple of years older than the boys she normally hung out with, which meant he was taller, and broader, and bigger all over. He even had the beginnings of a beard. He also had a girlfriend.

Gina loved him from afar, until the girlfriend got dropped, and then she loved him up close. As often as she could. At parties, weekends away, swimming at a friend's pool. They were never officially together. Not at first. But if they were at the same place at the same time, they always found their way into each other's arms. Greg said Gina was too young for a serious relationship, usually during some innocent fumbling around in the dark at some party. But, by the time he was nineteen and Gina seventeen, they were inseparable. So, they became a couple, and Gina thought she'd die from happiness.

Until Greg's uncle opened a dessert restaurant in Melbourne and Greg moved there to learn the trade. Before long he was appearing on television, delighting audiences with his cheeky charm. His youth, beauty, and talent for creating mouth-watering chocolate treats made him the talk of the town.

They broke up the day before Gina turned twenty. She knew it was coming. They talked it through. The long-distance thing would never work. But it didn't make it any less painful. She still got a stabbing ache in her chest when she thought of it.

Her phone rang, and she jumped out of her skin.

"Your guest is here," the production assistant said.

Gina's stomach flipped.

"Look at you, the New York City TV producer," Greg said as Gina stepped into the green room.

Her breath hitched in her throat when he flashed her a glittering smile.

"Look at you, the celebrity chef," she replied, hoping she sounded like the confident person she currently wasn't.

"Who would've thought we'd be so successful when we were screaming around the Dargle motocross track or getting busted by Mrs B making out in the back of my van."

He arched one eyebrow.

"Not Mrs B, that's for sure." Gina said, and when he threw his head back and laughed, a warm tingle rushed through her entire body.

He walked across the room and pulled her into his arms like it was the most natural thing in the world. Like they had seen each other yesterday.

"I've missed you, G," he whispered in her ear. "So much."

His warm breath tickled her cheek and a pleasant rush of goosebumps rippled across her skin.

His hair was still long, with unruly black curls tangled around the nape of his neck, and his eyes were still the bluest she had ever seen. He was just as beautiful as she remembered. But in the years since they parted, he had lost the prettiness of the boy, transforming into a stunningly handsome man.

He stepped back and cast an appraising eye over her, his hands resting on her shoulders. "New York agrees with you. You're a knockout."

Her heart thundered in her chest. "Thanks," she squeaked.

"This is Josie," he said, pointing to a petite woman on the sofa. "My publicist. But don't let her scare you. I'll talk about anything you want."

"Except anything personal," Josie said, with a cool smile.

"Oh yeah, I'm not allowed to talk about the Sadie break-up. She'll sue or something."

"You broke up?" Gina said, hearing an awkward crack in her voice.

"I said I can't talk about it." He winked. "But maybe we can catch up? Tonight, if you're not busy and you can ask me anything personal you want over – dinner?"

He gazed at her, expectantly.

"You've got the Barnes & Noble cocktail party tonight," Josie said without looking up from her phone.

His smile vanished. "Right. Damn."

There was a beat of silence in the room.

Gina shook her head as she tried to regain focus – her mind still swimming in his ocean-coloured eyes.

"Anyway," she said, after a deep and centring breath. "I have a few ideas for today's segment. Obviously, you're going to cook. We set everything up to your specifications. But I thought you could tell some stories from back home. I put down a few ideas." She handed him a piece of paper.

"Okay, sure," he said, not looking at it. "So, if we can't do dinner, would you want to come to the cocktail thing? I'd love to spend some time with you. I mean, if you're – available?"

He left the word 'available' dangling.

Josie stood up. "God, Greg. For someone so hot, you're useless." She turned to Gina. "I think he's asking if you have a boyfriend or anything. Or maybe he's just asking you to the cocktail party. Who can tell? I can have a ticket sent over, if you like?" She smiled another cool smile. The kind that showed no teeth.

Heat rushed into Gina's cheeks. "I, ah. I..."

"I'll send one over," Josie said. She turned to Greg. "I'm going to check the set. Don't do anything stupid while I'm gone," and she sashayed from the room, her sky-high heels clicking on the polished concrete floor.

"She's – nice?" Gina said.

"She's great. She just hides it well. She makes sure I always look good. It's a full-time job."

"I find that hard to believe," Gina muttered as she shuffled through her notes. She heard Greg laugh.

"So, er, *are* you seeing anyone?" he asked as he flopped down on the sofa. "I know I'm being nosey, but I've lost touch with most people from when we were – together, and we're old friends so..." He looked up at Gina, his blue eyes shining through jet black lashes.

Gina gulped.

"No. Not at the moment," she said as casually as she could. "Can we please go over the segment? It's important. I'll be in so much trouble if I screw it up."

"Will you come to the cocktail party?"

Her brows furrowed. "Are you giving me an ultimatum?"

He shot his palms up in mock surrender. "Whoa. Not at all. I just wanted to know if you'd like to come. Sorry. I'm being an idiot. Let's go over our segment."

She puffed out a deep sigh and dropped onto the sofa beside him. "I have to get up early, so I couldn't stay long."

He beamed at her. "That's okay. That's great. I'll get Josie to send through the details. Should I send a car? I'll send a car."

"I can get there on my own," she said with a laugh. "Can we talk work now?"

"I'm all yours," he said, and smiled.

CRIGO

Gina arrived at the venue for Greg's book launch and made her way towards the buzz of voices and clinking glasses. She stopped in front of a giant photo of Greg. He was wearing a tight white t-shirt and black jeans, with a crooked grin that revealed one deep dimple, and a smear of chocolate across his face. Over the photo it said, "Greg James, Australia's tastiest export."

She laughed, then sighed and then laughed again.

Taking a quick glance in a conveniently positioned ornate mirror, she smoothed down the front of her sparkly black mini dress, checked her boots for mud and tousled her hair. Then, drawing an embarrassingly shaky breath, she stepped through the door.

She spotted him instantly, not just because of the small crowd gathered around him, but because he stood at least a head taller than most people in the room.

He looked up, as if he sensed her entrance, and gave her a little wave. She waved back and then watched as he excused himself and strode towards her.

"You look amazing, G," he said as he leaned down and kissed her cheek. "And I love your hair like this." He twisted his finger in a red ringlet she'd spent way too long perfecting.

"Thanks," she said. "You look amazing too." He was wearing a cobalt blue suit that perfectly matched his eyes.

"You want to get out of here?" he said, grabbing her hand.

"We can't leave. This is your party."

"They're just here for free booze and my cakes and stuff. And as it's my party, I can do whatever I want." He gazed down at her. "Oh, god. I'm being an idiot again. You want to stay."

"No. I don't care about parties."

"Great," he said as he led her out of the room. "Because I have a surprise for you."

On the way out the door, a photographer stopped them. "One photo, Mr James?"

Gina went to pull away, but Greg drew her into him, his arm tightly wrapped around her waist.

"And your friend's name?" the photographer asked. "For the caption."

"Gina Morgan," Greg said. "My first love."

CRBD

Greg unlocked the door to *Chocolat and Moi*. "This is my buddy's place. It's closed tonight because his chef's getting married."

"What are we doing here?" Gina asked, as Greg flicked on the lights.

"I'm going to cook for you." He peeled off his jacket and tossed it over a chair. Stepping behind the bar, he picked out a bottle of champagne, and popped the cork into the air with a wide grin. "Come on," he said, passing Gina a glass and taking her by the hand.

She followed him into the kitchen. "What are you making?"

He unbuttoned his cuffs and pushed up his sleeves. "Buttermilk doughnuts with a whisky chocolate glaze."

Gina watched on as Greg cooked. It looked so effortless. The way he whipped the batter, his forearm flexing; the way he grated the chocolate, his shirt pulled tight across his chest. It was all she could do not to drool.

They chatted about their families, their lives, and about their past. Every so often he'd hold out a dripping spoon for her to try. Everything was delicious. Including him.

When he finally slid the tray into the oven, he turned and gave her a smile that almost swallowed her whole.

"What shall we do now," he said, moving over to her and weaving a hand across her hip.

"This," Gina said, and pressed her lips to his.

Greg had learned a lot about kissing in the years since they last saw each other. The hasty sloppiness of youth was replaced by a confident, eager expertise. His lips, still pillowy soft, moved on hers with surety, and when his tongue entered her mouth, she saw stars.

The oven dinged and Greg pulled away. "Damn timer," he said. He kissed her on the tip of her nose. "How about I ice these suckers and we take them to go?"

"That sounds perfect," she said with a slight quiver in her voice.

He looked at her with a soft smile. "I've missed you. I think about you all the time. I should never have let you go."

"We were kids," Gina said, more wisely than she felt. Her heart was pounding so hard, she thought it might burst from her chest, and the sweet aroma wafting from the oven was making her head swim.

"Well, we're not kids anymore," Greg said, a chocolate dripping spatula suspended in his hand.

Gina leaned across the counter, dipped her finger in the bowl of chocolate glaze and smeared it across her lips. "No. Not anymore," she said, and pressed her chocolate coated mouth to his.

Gina stretched – her arms up above her head, her toes pushing out from under the sheets. She ran her tongue around her lips and giggled, still tasting the sweetness of Greg and his luscious dessert.

Greg shifted beside her and guided her into his muscular arms. She traced a finger along his bicep, caressing his smooth, hot skin. He rolled on top of her, hovering above her, supporting his weight on his elbows, as he leaned down and kissed her deep and wet and hungry.

"Morning," she said when they finally came up for air.

Greg smiled, all sleepy and mussed up hair. "You fancy breakfast? Or…"

"Or, please," she said as she stretched up to kiss him again. She stopped short. "Wait, what time is it?"

"Time for this," he said, and pressed his lips to hers.

She returned the kiss, while not so subtly reaching for her phone. He chuckled into her mouth, and she drew away and checked the time. "Oh, god. I'm so late."

"I'm not letting you go to work on an empty stomach. I'm thinking chocolate chip pancakes." He slid out of bed and wandered naked across the room.

Gina stopped what she was doing and watched.

"Stop looking at my butt," he said over his shoulder.

"Then stop showing it to me."

He laughed as he stepped into the bathroom and kicked the door closed behind him.

Gina sat up and pulled a blanket around her as she looked at her messages. There were two from Tessa. She closed her eyes and groaned. The first was a text that said simply, *"You're late."* The second was a link to an article, with a photo of Greg and Gina and the caption, *'Chef's First Love Even Sweeter Than Chocolate.'*

Gina called the office.

"Tessa, I'm so sorry. I won't be long."

"Is your *childhood friend* still with you?" Tessa said, sarcasm dripping through the phone.

Gina winced. "Um. Yes."

Tessa sighed. "Gina, take the day off. Catch up, or whatever it is you two are doing. But tomorrow, you better be here early. And stay late."

"Thank you, Tessa."

"Mm," Tessa grumbled. "Tell him he can thank me by making me one of his famous desserts."

Greg emerged from the bathroom, clad in snug boxer briefs. "Did I get you in trouble?"

"It's not the first time."

He laughed. "No, I guess it's not." He sauntered across the room. "And hopefully, it won't be the last. I was thinking I might hang around for a while. If that's okay with you?"

She pulled him towards her.

He kissed her lightly, his lips softly brushing hers, the sweetness of last night's chocolate still magically lingering on his mouth.

"Do you always taste like chocolate," she said as she gazed up into his eyes.

"You'll have to keep kissing me to find out," he said, and gently bit her bottom lip.

9
SO MELTS HER HEART

KYLIE JACOBS

Part One

hat brings you here?" He smiled as he sat next to the attractive stranger with the warm chocolate eyes.

She looked up at him and hesitated only for a moment. "Same as you," she smiled back. "Just waiting." They were both conscious of the time.

"Hmmm." He looked back out the window into the sunny street, watching the bustling shoppers scurry along. "It is certainly warming up."

"It is, isn't it?" Her voice was like soft velvet when she spoke. "I've never been one for warm weather." She noticed his dark hair and gentle smile.

The minutes passed quickly as they sat next to each other, each of them feeling a little lost and anxious. Despite their constant distraction by the clock on the wall nearby, they began to enjoy the quiet as the lunchtime rush started to thin. "Are you waiting for someone in particular?" he asked.

"Why, yes." She smiled slightly. "I'm getting picked up by someone soon. They were supposed to be here by now. I can't help but wonder if they have forgotten me."

"I'm the same. My ride should come along any moment now. I would be happy to keep you company, though, if you don't mind me next to you." He slid toward her just a smidge, barely undetected, but enough to make her smile a little more. It made him realise his bold move was a safe one. "I haven't seen you in here before."

"I'm new. Well, new-ish,"

"Not me," he said proudly. "I've been here a while. I think a whole week if my thoughts are correct."

"A whole week." Her eyes widened. "I was just getting used to the place before I intended to leave." The familiar smells of chocolate and a hint of coffee in the air seemed to soothe her. The sunshine, that was lovely that morning, became a little uncomfortable as the time ticked by. "I would have liked to have stayed longer, but not here in the sun. What's it like here?"

"It's a nice place. I normally keep to myself and watch the children in and out with their families. I've made a few friends, but they don't stick around for too long."

"Do you ever get lonely?"

"Oh, gosh no. There is too much to look at, too much to take in. And now, here you are." His face brightened.

"Yes, here I am." She looked back over her shoulder at the room behind her. The crowd near the counter seemed to pay no attention to them sitting near the window, looking a little out of place. "They're a busy lot here, but they all seem friendly enough."

"I hope you don't mind me saying, but are you ok? You seem to be a little sad around the eyes."

She stopped for a moment and looked back out the window.

Without a word, her hand fell to her side, landing next to his with only a hair's width between them.

He quickly looked down, almost surprised at her forwardness.

"I'm sorry," she said, not pulling back. "I don't want to embarrass you or come across too strong, but I feel like we might be in a bit of a – a situation."

"A situation?"

"You can't feel it? You don't think something is happening between us? Something – strange?"

His smile faded slowly, and he looked down to see his hand moulding to hers. Almost embarrassed, he hesitated but didn't pull away. "I'm sorry. I didn't even realise."

"I knew it wasn't just me. It's okay." A tear formed in her eyes as she slid closer to him.

"I think the heat is getting to me." He looked out the window with anticipation. "My ride should be here any minute."

"I hope not." She sighed. She held his gaze, then slowly leaned further toward him, their shoulders pressing together. "Is this what it means to be powerless to a connection between two strangers? To feel it happening yet not having the ability to stop it if you wanted? Or losing the time to enjoy it?" She looked at the clock on the wall again.

"I don't mind this." He smiled slowly at her. "You. Dare I say. I cannot think of any place I would rather be right now. Knowing I'm comforting you, connecting with you, enjoying your company."

She bowed her head and sniffled softly.

"Please don't cry." He couldn't ignore the pain he heard. "We'll be out of here soon. You'll be okay." He felt himself pulling toward her. "Look! Here comes a car now. I bet it's for you." He tried to perk her up, but he couldn't hide the flattening of his own smile.

For a moment, she wondered. The glimmer in her eyes, though only present for a moment, was worth his attempt to console her. The car never slowed, never looked their way, never acknowledged they even existed. And her glimmer of hope was gone.

Another tear slid down her cheek as she looked down at their legs, now pressed together. "I'm not crowding you, am I?" Her tone was shaky. "I suppose, with the thought of you about to leave, I just feel a little uneasy about being left alone."

"It's okay. I'll wait right here with you," he said as the sun continued to warm and beat down on them through the window. "I won't leave your side. I promise."

Keeping an eye on the street for their rides, they felt the connection between them strengthen, drawing them closer to each other. Knowing they would soon have to part only made it more difficult to keep the conversation going. She was becoming a part of him, and she worried that being pulled apart would destroy her.

It wasn't long before their chatter and undeniable attraction drew them even closer. They both relaxed and leaned against the wooden ledge behind them. Feeling tired and abandoned, the afternoon sunshine began to fade to summer dusk, prompting them both to indulge in closing their eyes, moving even closer together. Hands intertwined, sides and legs pressed together, foreheads comforting each other as time pushed onward. Neither he nor she had ever felt so close to anyone else before. Despite being a new liaison, they valued their time together, knowing full well it was short-lived.

As the day marched through the late afternoon and well into the night, they fell into a soft, deep sleep, still intertwined with each other. No one woke them. The shopkeeper whistled as he cleaned up from the day's activities, the lights went out, and the door closed them inside, the lock clicking softly before silence took over their surroundings.

ᐸᔓᔓᐳ

Part Two

The next morning the children who were supposed to have collected their rare chocolate dolls, arrived to find them both still leaning against each other, resting as they faced the front window, still in their beautiful packaging, but now melted together into a lump, almost unrecognisable and certainly no longer beautifully crafted.

"Just as I suspected!" she spat. A large, stately woman with two young daughters entered The Chocolatier Café. "How could you children leave those lovely chocolate dolls near the window yesterday?" scolded their mother. With their young lips beginning to quiver, she continued, "This is your responsibility, and why play with them over there in the window? The shopkeeper didn't notice them left over there, nor should it be his responsibility to notice! How could you leave them behind? And so expensive. I don't know what I was thinking..."

The shopkeeper perked up, hearing the scolding float through the café. The embarrassed and sad children kept their heads down, trying to weather the storm. "What seems to be the problem, madam?" He scurried from around the counter to the window where they stood. "My, my." He stood shaking his head, pressing his palms to his cheeks as he looked at the discouraging circumstance. "This just cannot be. I thought you had taken them home. With such a hot day, they seem to have melted quite a bit."

"A bit?" the mother scoffed. "Why, you can't even recognise what they once were. It's a terrible mess, if you ask me."

"I don't suppose you still want them?"

"I'm sorry, despite the quality, but I certainly won't be taking them. Children with such neglect and utter nonsense should not be rewarded by sweets in any shape or form!"

Both children stood over the deformed chocolate dolls, teary-eyed and pouty, contemplating how they might solve the problem of convincing their mother they still deserved them. It wasn't long before the eldest daughter twisted her lips up to her nose in judgement. "Who'd want them now anyway," she whispered into the curls of her little sister's hair. "I wouldn't even know where to start with a lump of chocolate like that."

"Yes, we'll just leave them," the mother snapped, feeling her spoilt children had learnt no lesson. "We'll be off now. Nothing for either of you." She turned her attention to the shopkeeper, shaking her head in frustration. "May I leave this with you?" She waved her long, manicured finger like a wand over the small, darkened mess in the window. Pulling on their arms, she marched the young girls out of the shop with the ongoing reprimanding fading into the street. "All that money. You both don't deserve such lovely treats. The way you just left them there..."

The shopkeeper soon complemented his frown with quiet mumblings as he promptly scooped up the package, now smeared with melted chocolate. Under his breath, "Leave them with me? I insist that you do."

After the upset children left the shop empty-handed and their mother's nagging still ringing in his ears, the shopkeeper looked down at the deformed chocolate and shook his head, sadness filling his heart. He placed it on the counter and carefully opened the pretty packaging. Peeling it back gently, he cocked his head, his thoughts filling with ideas for the beautiful dark chocolate. He picked up his scalpel and carefully removed the uneven, candied features of their faces. He noticed their hands still fused together and he smiled, an idea forming in his mind. He slipped them into his refrigerator and when the time was appropriate, he began to work his magic. Moulding here and melting there, carving this, and smoothing that, he worked exceptionally for the next two hours, saving only the hands of a short-lived love. Resting back on his stool, he smiled as he stole a moment to enjoy what he had created.

The moment he set it in his display cooler, the front door opened with the ring of a bell. "Good afternoon." He smiled as a young couple walked toward him, their hands intertwined, swinging together. "What can I do for you?"

"We are looking for something to commemorate this special day." He smiled, his eyes soaking her in.

"What's so special about this day?" she giggled, slapping his arm playfully.

"You'll just have to wait and see." He raised her hand to his lips and kissed her like a princess. "She loves dark chocolate," he continued, gazing into her pretty face. "It is her absolute favourite."

"I have just the thing." The shopkeeper went back to the display cooler and lifted his newest creation out, carrying it to the couple and placing it in front of them for their viewing and approval.

She gasped and covered her mouth with her delicate fingers. "I love it!" The young woman pressed her hands to her chest as she leaned in to marvel over the heart-shaped chocolate hollowed out to show two small, detailed hands, lovingly clasped together inside. She bent even closer. Her eyes seem to smile as she followed the carvings and symbols. "The intricate detail is incredible and it's – extraordinary. I can feel the love when I look at it. We just have to have it," she exclaimed standing up straight. "Don't you think? We just have to. Please?" She soon held her lover's hand between both of hers, eyes wide and pleading like an innocent child.

"No matter the cost," he answered tenderly, taking only a moment to glance and nod at the shopkeeper.

"Wonderful." The shopkeeper smiled proudly. Payment was made and he wrapped the creation beautifully, with satin ribbon and gold tape. "Be sure to keep it cool." He felt he had to mention, before gently sliding it across the counter toward the awaiting, doe-eyed girl. Looking over her shoulder, "If you don't mind me asking, what *does* make this day so special?"

"This," the boy said, causing the curious girl to pivot around, unprepared. He held her hands to her sides, then lowered himself to his knee before her. Then, reaching into his pocket, fumbling for a moment, he managed to nervously pull out a small black box. Holding it up towards her gaping mouth, his voice trembled, which suited the worry on his face. "You have made me the happiest man in the world the day I met you, Maggie. Will you marry me?"

She squealed, pulled him up with unladylike strength, then strangled his neck tightly, and in moments her acceptance was soon repeated over and over through tears of joy.

The shopkeeper smiled, as the young couple melted into each other's arms. Turning to the counter, he looked down at the chocolate hands intertwined inside the heart, their hold seemingly tightening. This time his creation wasn't creating tears of regret, but tears of joy. A sweet creation that was once deemed disrespected and unworthy, was now deemed the most precious chocolate treat of all.

10
LOVING THE ALIEN
J A MACNALLY

For a fleeting moment as he glanced out the porthole window, he could almost believe he was storm-tossed on an ocean somewhere in the blackest depths of night. There were no familiar landmarks or guiding lights, and even the stars seemed to have lost their glow.

He had never felt more alone, more isolated.

He wondered if this was the end for him.

For the seventeenth 'morning' he dutifully opened his onboard log to record his last known position – a guess, since the navi-computer and radar array had both been destroyed during the massive debris collision, and only the Maker knew how far off course he'd drifted since then. He worked his way down the list of standard check points as a way of maintaining normality, just as though he wasn't teetering on the brink of death. Life in space had taught him the importance of always following rules and procedures, since any tiny mistake could prove fatal, and routine was all he had to cling to now.

In terms of life support, he noted this as marginal since the oxygen supply was getting uncomfortably low. An earlier check had revealed that the old filters were struggling to clean the carbon dioxide out of the atmosphere properly and looked on the verge of packing it in all together soon. He'd had to reduce heating to a bare minimum to conserve the remaining power, after one of the two solar panels was shattered in the collision. As for food stores, there were enough freeze-dried basic proteins and carbs to last a while, but little in the way of what passed for stimulants or indulgent items. There was enough recycled water, so he didn't need to ration that just yet. The water would last longer than his body's resistance to freezing, but that was scant comfort.

He checked communications and frowned, puzzled that the comms appeared to be working but all he got was static, but never a response to his constant, automated maydays.

Having completed the official part of his log duties, he opened a new entry to record a private supplement. Personal entries were not looked on favourably by Command, but as he was probably going to die out here anyway, the planet-bound brass could kiss his frozen butt. He'd decided yesterday, during a bleak moment of reflection, that he didn't want his death to be just another anonymous space statistic, so whoever found this recording should know he had been someone – a son, brother, friend, or colleague.

He rubbed his cold hands over his bristly cheeks, wondering what to say.

"This is Captain Thomas Davidson of the deep space explorer Guylién, personal log supplemental. It's been seventeen solar days now since my ship was hit by a previously uncharted cloud of space debris. It knocked out my nav computer and radar array, so I have no way of knowing how far off course I was thrown, or where I am now. I assume I'm not near one of the normal navigation lanes or I would've been spotted by now. I was a long way out when my ship was hit, returning from a deep space exploratory mission. There's very little power left, so I don't imagine I'll last more than a few days, maybe a week if I'm lucky."

He paused, his brow furrowing as he struggled to maintain a stoic front despite the growing despair that threatened to overwhelm him.

"It's tough, being so far off course, knowing I probably won't be found in time. I'll try to keep going as long as I can. At least my core samples and all that damned analysis is preserved for my fellow geo guys to drool over one day. I'd kill for a decent cup of hot coffee right now, with one of those dark chocolates my mum used to send me on my birthday. Man, that chocolate was unreal. Anyway," he cleared his throat, refocusing his grey eyes in the dim emergency lights, "I'll check comms again; see if anyone can hear me. The transponder signal should be working unless it's been knocked out, along with practically everything else on this bucket. Tom Davidson signing off."

C3&0

It was the sound of a quiet, repetitive voice that woke Tom from his uneasy sleep a few hours later. He'd been lying slumped sideways in his padded pilot's seat, dreaming of floating in coffee, smelling the heady, chocolatey fragrance as the liquid tossed him lightly this way and that.

He groped towards the comms button automatically, never so deeply asleep that he couldn't wake up quickly, if required.

"Captain Thomas Davidson of the explorer vessel Guylién reporting. Respond."

There was a loud burst of static and then that quiet, flat voice again, saying, "I read you, Captain. I have located your ship, accessed your logs, and confirmed your identity. According to your mission plan, you are well off course."

He grunted, bemused by the brisk summary. "Just a bit. I've lost nav and radar so don't know where I am."

"Just a moment. I can provide you with your current location." He glanced down at the com screen and noticed that the speaker had already downloaded the coordinates.

"Fuck it, I'm nowhere near any navigable lanes," he cursed, then added apologetically, "Pardon my French."

"Your French, Captain? According to the personnel records, you are originally from old Terra, on the American continent."

"It's just a saying when people swear. Where are you from, if not old Terra?"

The reply came slowly after a noticeable pause. "I – originate – from Ganymede."

"So, you're a long way from home, too. Where are you stationed now?" He was so relieved to be talking to another person, to know that someone, somewhere, knew he was still alive that he felt an almost giddy rush of adrenaline warming its way through his veins.

"I am on the Outer Rim orbital station Omnomia. Our powerful deep space comms network enabled me to detect your signal, weak though it is. I am working to locate the nearest vessel that can be diverted to rescue you."

"Sweet Mary, mother of God, you've no idea how glad I am to hear you say that."

"My name is not Mary, Captain. My designation is Comms and Research Officer. You may call me Vira."

"Okay – Vira." He paused, aware now the voice sounded

gentler, more feminine. He wondered whether Standard was her first language since she seemed to take what he said so literally. "Thank you, by the way, for finding me. I'd just about given up hope." He bit his lip, afraid to say more, in case he admitted he had given up hope of ever setting foot on solid ground once more, breathing real atmosphere, being warm again, or seeing and touching another person.

"You are welcome, Captain. I was accessing deep range probes out this way, so it was serendipitous that I located your signal." Her formal reply seemed to rebuff his thanks, but he'd take her standoffish attitude over never hearing another voice again. She added briskly, "Comms contact will be lost for approximately five hours while my station is in the orbital shadow of the primary planet. I will resume contact with you when the station clears the planet, and your vessel is in range again."

"Five hours seems a long time just to twiddle my thumbs," he joked weakly, shivering involuntarily from the increasing cold.

"I suggest you try to rest as much as possible to conserve your remaining strength. Ending communication now."

The ensuing hiss of static sounded unbearably loud in the cramped confines of the tiny cabin, but it was the only lifeline he had so he left it on. Quivering from the cold, and perhaps reaction, he tugged his padded thermal jacket closer around his body, adjusted the wrap of his thermal outer blanket and shut his eyes, hoping he'd dream of Vira, or if not her, then maybe a freshly brewed mocha coffee topped with premium chocolate shavings, his favourite brew when in port.

"Captain Davidson, are you receiving me?"

Tom jerked awake, his mouth dry and his heart pounding at the sound of a real voice, not something from one of his video feeds. "Yes, I'm here, Vira. I must have dozed off." In truth he'd been dozing on and off for a few hours, his body starting to shut down from the continued freezing conditions inside the cabin. "I thought maybe you'd forgotten about me."

"That is most unlikely, Captain. A vessel has been diverted to intercept your orbit, but it will not reach you for approximately twenty hours. You must try harder to conserve your power supply."

Tom managed a dry laugh, but it emerged as a croak. "I don't know what else I can do, Vira. I'm already freezing my butt off, eating cold provisions, and I've shut down non-essential areas of the ship, so I'm basically confined to the main cabin. I'd say it was cosy, if only I had heating."

"All your precautionary measures will help," Vira replied in a tone that was almost rallying.

"I'm not meaning to be pessimistic but I'm not sure I'll last another twenty hours at this rate. There's core samples from my exploratory work analysed and stored, so whoever rescues me must salvage that, and then it won't be a complete waste."

At least then his death would still count for something.

His breath formed icy particles in front of his face as he spoke, and he felt his eyeballs starting to freeze as well. Great, he thought, I'm going to end up blind as well as being a human icy pole.

"Do not give up hope, Captain. Based on your personnel file, you have a great deal of resilience and determination to survive. Your interest in geology – this is a life-long interest, not merely a professional one?"

Tom was surprised by her personal question. "Yeah. I've

always been interested in the history of planets, their geological features, right from my childhood when my folks dragged me off to explore archaeological digs. It became a passion, being the first person to set foot on a planetoid or meteor, discovering its origins. That's a thrill I never tire of." He paused, aware he had revealed far more than he'd intended.

"Your work will not be wasted. You will be rescued. You must believe this, Captain," Vira replied, sounding more encouraging. "I am ending communications now. Next check-in will be in five hours."

⊂ℨ∞⊃

"What do you do when you're off duty?" Tom asked Vira near the end of their next check-in, curious to learn more about her.

"I do not stop working – ever."

"That's just sad."

"How is it different to you always being alone in space?"

"You got me. Seems we have lots in common."

"Less than you think, Captain. Transmission ending now."

⊂ℨ∞⊃

"Captain, how are you?" Vira asked at their next check-in, and her voice sounded warmer, even caring.

"It's getting harder to stay focused. Sorry to disappoint you but I don't think I'll last until the rescue ship gets here."

"I am certain you will. Concentrate on staying alive, on what you will most look forward to when you are rescued," Vira said encouragingly. Was it his imagination or did she sound a lot friendlier?

"What I want more than anything right now is a hot coffee."

"Coffee?" she echoed in disbelief.

"Yep, the good stuff, freshly pressed like Kenyan Volcanica coffee but mocha style," he murmured dreamily, almost feeling a bit thawed just imagining the smell and taste of the expensive, delicious blend.

"Mocha? That is not from coffee beans, but cacao beans?" she clarified, her soft voice with its lilting upward inflection sounding like melted chocolate poured over vanilla bean ice cream – another favourite from his childhood.

"Mmm, chocolate. Every year on my birthday my mum sends me a package of the good stuff. It costs her a fortune, but she hates the thought of me out here all alone, doing what I love but not able to indulge my addiction. When I'm in port I head straight to a bar to order a real coffee, and then I add some shaved chocolate. Food of the gods, it used to be called. What's your poison?"

"Poison? I do not ingest poison, Captain," she replied reprovingly.

Tom smiled in the cold darkness. "Sorry, it's a Terran expression meaning what's your favourite drink, normally something alcoholic. When this is over I'd like to shout you to whatever you like," he offered, aware he wanted to meet her, to thank the person who had found him – provided he survived long enough for the rescue vessel to reach him.

"I do not think it will be possible for us to meet, Captain, but thank you for the offer." Her voice had lowered, become huskier, and he wondered again if he was imagining it was richer, deeper, more like liquid chocolate to match his cravings.

"What – you never even get shore leave? Your boss must be a slave driver."

"Not at all. Professor Teuscher is a brilliant, dedicated scientist and it is my honour to assist her."

"Sorry. I meant no offence. All the same, I'd like to meet you one day, just to say thank you for finding me, keeping me sane." Tom's voice also lowered, but his huskiness was the result of being almost frozen. She probably thinks I'm a lunatic, he thought wryly.

"I hope our conversations have helped keep you focused on surviving. You do not sound insane."

"Ah, not yet, but the day is young," he teased.

There was a slight pause before she replied in a tone he swore was equally playful, "Another attempt at levity, Captain?"

"Yeah, and how about you call me Tom? I think we're way past being so formal."

"Indeed – Tom. Unfortunately, we're almost out of range again. We'll speak soon when you reach my station. Try to rest, and dream of your hot chocolate."

"It's coffee with melted chocolate, actually, but I'll try. Good night, Vira."

"Good night, Tom. I would dream of chocolate if I could."

Her last words were just a murmur, so soft he wasn't sure he'd heard them properly, if at all.

CB∂O

Tom missed out speaking with Vira by the time his ship was in comms range. She spoke to him urgently to let him know the rescue vessel was approaching, but he'd fallen into a hypothermic coma and couldn't hear her. He awoke a few days later in the medical facility on the Outer Rim orbital station Omnomia where Vira was stationed, sufficiently recovered to log a call to the Comms and Research Division, hoping to speak to her. The technician on duty said crisply, "There is no one here by that name, Captain."

"But she said she worked here, for Professor Teuscher, I think," Tom replied, trying not to sound disappointed. They had only talked a handful of times after all, barely enough to count as anything meaningful, but her voice had become his lifeline.

The technician placed him on hold then another voice came online saying in an oddly familiar yet formal tone, "Captain Davidson, I am Professor Maribel Teuscher, Vira's – er – supervisor. If you are well enough, please come to my lab and I will explain what I can."

ೞೲ

Professor Teuscher's lab was like something out of a bad science fiction vid show – all gleaming chrome, glass walls and tendrils of light. The professor herself was another surprise: short, slender, with auburn hair and the biggest, brownest eyes he'd ever seen, like melted milk chocolate.

When she spoke, he started in surprise because her voice was so like Vira's, the way it had been during their early exchanges. "I apologise that Vira is not able to meet you personally."

Tom wondered if Vira was shy or didn't want to offend him

by turning him down in person, but his need to see her had become a compulsion. "I know I only had a handful of conversations with her, but I thought... I'm sorry if I came on too strong, scared her off, but I just wanted to see her, to thank her for finding me out there. I'd have died without her."

"The reason you cannot meet her is because... here, let me show you."

She touched a high-tech computer screen, and Tom scowled suspiciously at this delaying tactic.

"This is Vira," the professor said, indicating a shimmering pattern of dancing lights on the screen, "short for Voice Recognition, designed to undertake deep space exploratory missions using existing networks, similar to piggy-backing onto satellites to increase her range. She discovered you quite by chance, and having analysed your personnel files, adjusted her interaction to help you stay alive. She's evolving, so she tried to become what you needed and wanted."

Tom's mouth opened and closed soundlessly. "You sound just like her."

Maribel smiled self-consciously. "I had no-one else around when I first developed Vira, so I had to use my voice for testing. I keep meaning to change it."

"Don't," he said impulsively. "It's a lovely voice. Once she started talking that way, like melted chocolate, that helped – a lot."

Maribel smiled more easily now. "Okay. Well, I'm finished for the day. Would you like to join me for a drink? I'd like to tell you more about Vira, and you can tell me about your work."

"Sure. What's your poison?" Tom asked without thinking.

She removed her lab coat, saying, "Actually, I'm more in the mood for a café mocha. I get premium dark chocolate shipped out here as a perk of the job, if you'd like to share some?"

Tom smiled, craving the taste of chocolate, but also the company of this woman with the chocolate brown eyes and Vira's voice. "I'd like that, very much."

II

THE CHOCOLATE BOX

FIONA M MARSDEN

The bell over the shop door chimed and Ellie hurried from her workshop through to the counter. Business had been slow after the holiday season, and Valentine's Day was weeks away. She couldn't allow a customer to leave without some small purchase of chocolate to put a few coins in the till. The day was almost done and only a handful of shillings graced the coffers.

Her breath hitched. A tall figure studied the blocks of chocolate, occasionally picking one from the shelves in gloved hands to study the label and placing it back down precisely. He wore civilian clothes under a long navy coat that would be ideal against the blustery cold of the London streets in January. As much as anything it proved him a man of means, many of his less fortunate contemporaries were still relying on army issue khaki trench coats three years after the armistice.

Ellie smoothed down her apron, wishing she'd chosen her ruby velvet today, instead of the everyday blue serge. Even if it matched her eyes. The bare head, with slightly ruffled blond hair was achingly familiar. Algernon Spalding, one of her most frequent customers since he walked into the shop in late November seeking Christmas gifts for his numerous sisters, cousins, and aunts. Reckoned by the dozens, if his ongoing purchases were any indication. She didn't like to think how many of the pretty boxes were for a special woman in his life. Or women?

"Miss Palmer." He inclined his head, a slight tilt keeping the right side in shadow.

Breathlessness invaded her voice, the words coming out whispery and finishing on a squeak. "Mr Spalding. How can I assist you today?"

His double-breasted ulster was open at the front to show off his plain blue suit, white shirt and a narrow black tie. Not for him the frivolity of a knacky bow tie. A serious banker, she'd learned from something he'd said in one of the casual conversations he'd instigated when the shop had been empty of other customers. A family bank, so he would be assured of his position once he returned from the war.

He leaned over the glass topped counter, scrutinising the trays of individual chocolates on display. "What do you recommend?" His speech had an odd cadence that made her think of a boy with a mouthful of stolen chocolate trying not to give himself away.

"Is it for a lady?"

His head jerked up, revealing the side he usually kept hidden. Scarred soldiers were common on the streets of London these days. It was surprising to find a man so self-conscious about his damaged face. Though he must have been a very handsome man before something ripped a hole in his cheek and the doctors sewed it back together. It had resulted in a haphazard spiral of scars radiating from a divot. The hollowed flesh lay a knuckle length away from the corner of his mouth, leaving it slightly twisted in a permanent upward tilt. A clownish half smile if you will, but not unattractive. Perhaps the reason for the slow, imperfect speech.

He responded, meeting her eyes for the first time today. His were a warm chocolate, smooth and darker than usually seen in a fair Englishman, an extra scoop of cocoa beans added to the mix. "A lady friend."

She hid her disappointment. An aunt would have been more acceptable. "The violet creams are fresh made."

"The ones with the purple flowers? What are these with the pink petals?"

"Rose fondant."

He nodded, drawing his pocketbook from inside his coat.

"A mix of both. In a pretty box with a matching ribbon." He indicated the shelves behind the counter where she kept the specially made cardboard shapes.

"She must be a special friend." To warrant the most expensive chocolates in the most expensive box. Crystalised rose petals and violets were an expensive luxury in an English winter.

"A school friend of my... wife. Her birthday is tomorrow, and I must attend."

A wife existed, even if he stumbled over the word. Not surprising. He must be more than thirty years old, though the experiences of war aged those who went to the trenches beyond their years. In any case, many a married man lingered to flirt with shop girls. It meant little, and a girl would be a fool to take them seriously. Not that Mr Spalding flirted. There were no compliments and furtive touches. It was more a seeming lack of desire to leave the warm interior of the shop. She darted a glance at the failing light beyond the window, flurries of snow illuminated by the newly lit gas lamps.

It took only a minute or two to pack one of the pink and purple gift boxes with the chocolates and tie a pink bow around the middle to hold the lid in place. The wrapping was more complicated, requiring careful pleats and tucks to keep the heavy paper from crushing the ribbon.

He tendered a pound note and she eyed it warily, conscious of her small amount of change. She'd had to pay the rent this morning, so she had little in reserve.

His gloved hands closed over the note, and she hoped he might offer something smaller, perhaps a crown. She surely had five shillings in the till.

Instead, he lay the note on the counter. "I wonder if you might help me."

"Of course."

His brows drew together and his mouth too, as if he found it hard to find the words.

"I have a friend who is partial to nuts, but his injuries make it hard for him to chew. Is there something you have to give him the taste?"

"Without the effort? Of course. A paste made of peanuts would be simple to make."

"We have offered such a paste, but it clings."

A challenge indeed. "Perhaps mixed with a soft fondant. Some extra corn syrup or oil to ease it down."

"It would be appreciated. I will pay in advance, and you can send a batch of two dozen to my address by messenger."

"I'm pleased to be of service, sir."

His gaze warmed. "It will be a kindness for my friend."

She wondered if his friend were at the Queen's hospital where they treated the badly injured soldiers, but it wasn't her place to ask such a personal question. "Seeing it's a special order, I'll have to ask three shillings the dozen."

The money lay on the counter and still there would not be enough spent for her to give the gentleman his change.

"It sounds reasonable." He glanced around at the shelves. "If I'm to visit my friend, I should take something for the other patients."

At his insistence, she helped him choose a number of the chocolate blocks in different flavours. He stood close, keeping his injured face to the offside with obvious care. His scent was an odd mix of damp woollen coat, leather, and spice and, now and then as he moved, something warm and enticing.

Finally, the pencilled figures on the docket added up to a shilling short of the full pound.

"Keep it for the messenger. He'll deserve a bonus for venturing out in this weather."

He stood watching as she readied the parcels, tying the bundle up with string leaving extra to create a knotted handle, the precious beribboned box on the top. For a moment she thought he might say something momentous. His mouth curled up in a smile, reflecting the melting warmth of his eyes. Maybe the injury tugged, for he flinched and the expression in his eyes dulled.

"Thank you for your assistance, Miss Palmer."

Ellie watched him go out into the dark, pausing to button his coat in the shelter of the doorway. A kind man who exuded loneliness, even as he spoke of a wife. She folded the pound note into her purse. She would take it across to the post office in the morning to break into small change for the shop. She wondered which bank he worked at. A laugh forced its way from her tightened throat. It would be foolish to take her little sum to a bank in the City. They were not for the likes of a shopkeeper with a meagre few pounds in savings. The post office was easier.

Mr Spalding's house was only a short walk away from the high street where he came to purchase her chocolates, one of a dozen in a rather nice cul-de-sac. Ellie clasped the box of specially made peanut fondants and wondered if she should have sent young George around to do the delivery. Of all the houses, his appeared the most worn, the knocker a little tarnished and the step muddy with melted snow and dirt from the road. A pot beside the door held a dead shrub, a bare skeleton she suspected had not been a casualty this winter or the last.

Gripping the knocker, she beat a mild tattoo, losing her courage immediately. This was a mistake. Yesterday, their collaboration on creating something for his friend enthused her. Now it seemed encroaching to expect to see him personally. To have his opinion on her creation while she was present.

She was about to retreat when there was a fumble on the inside of the door and a young maid poked her nose around the barely opened portal. From the look of her damp apron, she'd come directly from the kitchen.

"What can I do for you, Miss?"

"Is Mr Spalding home? I have a delivery for him."

The door opened a fraction more. "A delivery? I don't know if I should accept it. They usually go round the back and cook takes it in."

"Would you like me to go to the rear entrance?"

The girl looked her up and down, obviously confused by the khaki greatcoat in partnership with Ellie's best hat trimmed with a bunch of cherries.

"I think I better let you inside and tell the master."

Ellie followed the maid into a dim hallway. She lay her hat on the dusty table near the front door after the girl swiped it quickly with her apron.

"I'll take your coat, shall I?"

Shedding her outer layer, Ellie took her time, admiring the layout of the hall but wondering at the worn carpet on the timber stairs and the obvious neglect. From his neat and well-dressed appearance, she would have expected Mr Spalding's house to be at least well kept.

"If you'll wait in here, Miss. I'll tell Mr Spalding you've arrived. Oh. I should tell him who, shouldn't I?"

Handing over her business card, Ellie stood in the middle of what must be the parlour as the girl bustled up the stairs. It had the same air of neglect as the hall, as if it were unused.

A selection of photographs on a piano drew her over. She'd always found photographs of families fascinating. She had so little family of her own, none at all since her brother died.

Tucked in the back, she found what she was unconsciously looking for. Mr Algernon Spalding and bride. They both looked very young, the bride's dress some years out of fashion. A war bride? She was tiny compared to her tall handsome husband, with lovely big eyes and a rosebud of a mouth.

It was a small photograph to one side that caused her heart to stumble. The bride again, this time with a young child. A little girl with her mother's eyes and mouth and her father's fair hair.

She looked around wildly, hoping for escape. She shouldn't have come.

◌੩੪◌

Algie glanced around the drawing room, seeing the dust and worn furnishings with fresh eyes. With her eyes. Lovely eyes that had looked at him like he was a man. Gave him hope.

How would she look now she'd seen his home? Three years of neglect. He'd not cared enough to replace the housekeeper. A pulse of anger jolted his heart into action. An unfamiliar sensation until these last few months. Not always anger, but feelings he didn't need or want. Her fault. Always her.

"What can I do for you, Miss Palmer?"

She held up a parcel, neatly tied up with string with the clever little handle. "Your order is ready."

"I expected a messenger boy to bring it. You shouldn't have come out of your way."

She stepped back, seeming startled by his aggressive tone. "I'm sorry. I meant to leave it at the door, but your maid seemed to think..." She waved one hand around in an oddly helpless gesture.

"Please don't apologise. It's I who should apologise. You were doing me a favour."

He took the parcel and looked around for somewhere to put it. The slight disarrangement of the photographs triggered a tightness in his gut. She'd been looking at them. He swivelled away and placed the chocolates on a small end table near the sofa.

There was an uncomfortable silence, and he searched for something to say. "May I offer you refreshments?"

"I was admiring your photographs. I hope..."

She stumbled to a halt as her words tangled with his and flushed a rich colour that echoed the red in her dress.

Algie inclined his head, keeping his scars slightly away. "Pray go ahead. You were saying?"

"Your photographs. I was admiring them while I waited. I hope you don't mind."

"Why should I?"

"I'm a shopkeeper. Not a guest."

"You could be. I offered you refreshment."

She glanced at the piano. "I shouldn't. Unless your wife is present."

"My wife is dead." He saw the questioning glance. "And my daughter."

"I'm so sorry." He could see her comprehension as she scanned the room with its unkempt appearance.

"We've all lost people. I'm sure you did also?" He made it a question, and she nodded.

"My brother died in the last days of the war."

"No-one else?"

"I had a sweetheart. I was barely sixteen and he looked grand in uniform. It was more a tragedy for his family."

He picked up the photograph of his wife and child, hardly able to remember the feelings he'd had for his hurried wartime bride. "I never met my daughter. She was born while I was in France and when I came back, my wife informed me I wasn't fit to be seen. By the time the doctors patched me up enough for polite society, the Spanish flu had taken them both." Taken the whole household. He looked up, hating the sympathy on his visitor's face. "I hardly knew them. I'm not a candidate for pity, Miss Palmer."

"In that case, why do you hide your scars?"

The blunt words struck home. "I don't know. Habit maybe?"

"Were they very bad?" Her soft tones soothed the spikey feelings he got when people looked at his face and arms. He automatically put his hands into his trouser pockets.

"Not as bad as some."

"Like your nut loving friend?"

"We were in the Air Force together. I got out of it lightly compared to Peter."

"I hope he likes his chocolates."

"I'm sure he will. Your chocolate boxes are great favourites with everyone."

"Do you really have so many sisters and cousins and aunts?"

She fixed her enquiring gaze on him, and a rush of blood heated his cheeks, a burning sensation around his scars where the skin was still fragile. "Not as many as you would expect."

ಛಾ೩೦

Ellie stared at the flush on his skin. Her enquiry embarrassed him? "Who do you give them to?"

"Girls at the bank. I do have relatives. I usually take some out to the hospital when I visit."

"And for birthdays." It was tonight, she suddenly recalled. She glanced at the grandfather clock beside the door. "I should be going so you can get ready."

"I'm ready now. I only need my overcoat and gloves. Nora is a friend of my sister, who will also be there tonight. They introduced me to my wife when I was on furlough in the summer of nineteen-fifteen. They both worry which is why I have to attend the party."

"Because you're alone."

His eyes darkened. "Because I'm alone."

"You should take a friend to the party. Then they wouldn't worry."

"Are you offering?" There was a hopeful tone in his voice.

Ellie indicated her velvet dress. It was her best, but not suitable for a fancy party. "I hardly think so."

"It's not that kind of party. More a family dinner and maybe some party games after. Charades and things. It could be fun if we went together."

She still felt doubtful. "I could always bring extra chocolates for the party."

"You would be popular with my sister. She dotes on your chocolates."

"Are you sure? Your sister might have other ideas."

"My sister and friends will be happy to see me out with someone."

"Any someone?"

"A pretty someone is always acceptable."

He thought she was pretty. Her whole body melted. "Could we go to the shop to pick up more chocolate?"

"I have a little motor so we can zip around in no time."

He helped her into her coat and waited while she pinned her hat in place.

"My dear Miss Palmer, you have no idea how much I'm looking forward to this party."

Strangely enough, she was looking forward to it too, despite feeling nervous about meeting his family and friends.

When they pulled up outside her shop, he touched her sleeve. "I was wondering. Would you like to motor out to Bexley on Sunday while I visit my friends? You don't have to come in if you'd rather not."

His deep chocolate-brown eyes searched her face intently, a small crease between his brows. He was inviting her to share in more than a simple drive. Hope warmed the lonely part of her soul.

"I'd love to come."

12
PIPPA'S SECRET
CLARE MILES

our choice," Jed said, pushing the chocolate box across the scarred wooden table towards her.

"No, it's your turn," Pippa replied, pushing it back.

"Ladies first," he insisted.

"Cut that crap. It's the final round and your turn."

Jed's eyes narrowed, turning almost navy. She thought she'd categorized every one of their changing shades, but she'd never seen them this dark. Then again, she'd never seen him like this, lit by flickering candlelight as day edged into night.

"I don't imagine Australia's finest university taught you to speak like that." His low rumble raced down her spine reaching the tips of her toes covered in two layers of his socks, grabbed from the boot of his car.

"There were lots of things it didn't teach me." Like how to outgrow a crush. One that kept a flush on her cheeks, despite the icy cottage they sat in.

He looked down at the chocolates and, if she ever needed a reminder that hers was a one-sided attraction, this was it. With frustrating calmness, he focused on the gold edged box. Finally, he reached in and picked one, the lid obscuring her view while he undid the wrapper. Pippa watched him take a bite with a flash of white teeth, and, somehow, she managed to hold back her moan. How could someone eating a chocolate look so absolutely delectable? Something she knew had nothing to do with her sugar addiction and everything to do with the man doing the eating.

"Pippa?"

"What?" she snapped realising she'd been staring. And worse, he'd noticed.

"Your guess?"

"Mint. It was mint," she threw out wildly. It could have been tar for all she'd noticed. All she could smell in the dank musty room, was him. A tantalizing mix of scents she'd know anywhere. Like he'd bottled water from the crystal-clear river that flowed nearby, and added some of the eucalyptus-scented air from the surrounding mountains, then finished with a dash of something wild and untamed, like him, and the rugged landscape he worked in, lived in, loved.

He smiled, the genuine one that crinkled his eyes and stole her breath. Every. Single. Time.

Reaching for her mug, she took a healthy slug of the only beverage they'd found in the pantry, a bottle of red wine, well past its prime. As the liquid roared down her throat, she wondered, not for the first time, when she'd outgrow these inconvenient feelings for him. Feelings which no amount of absence or time seemed to abate.

"Lucky." He opened his palm to display Mint labelled on the green foil.

"That's three correct answers from me, and none for you," she teased, keeping her tone light and playful. "Give up?"

"Never!"

An enormous gust of wind rattled the cottage and rain lashed the windows. She shivered, and hitched the blanket, also grabbed from his car, tighter around her shoulders.

"You cold?" he asked.

"If you try to give me your coat one more time ..."

"I'll put that on your gravestone – after you die from hypothermia."

She laughed. "Stop trying to distract me from the storm, and from this—" she waved an all-encompassing hand around the dilapidated room, "—monstrosity of mouldiness."

His echoing laugh wrapped around her, warming her far more than any blanket could. "Monstrosity of mouldiness. Chateau of shabbiness. Has anyone told you, you have a way with words?"

"Yeah. You."

C>ଚ

If I had a way with words, Jed thought, maybe I'd be able to figure out how to tell my boss's daughter I'm in love with her. He gave himself an imaginary upper cut. She'd definitely demonstrate her way with words if she heard him call her that. And rightly so. She was much more than his boss's daughter. He felt a smile form at the many ways he could describe her.

Independent. Definitely.

Smart. Undoubtedly.

Stubborn. Absolutely.

Sexy. Always.

No wonder she captivated him. Even now, after the day they'd had, and wrapped in layers of blankets, she should have had the grace to look at least marginally unappealing. Instead, the warmest brown eyes he'd ever seen sparkled at him over the top of her mug.

"You're staring. Is it my hair? Has it gone crazy curly again?" She pushed her hair behind an ear, in an endearing gesture she'd never outgrown.

"It's not crazy curly. It's wavy," he assured her, not for the first time. Free from the complicated style she'd worn this morning, it framed her face in a mass of curls that fell to her shoulders. Curls that she loathed but that had always tempted him to reach out and touch. He needed to know if they felt as soft as they looked. Not a good idea.

She scrunched up her face. "How much of that wine have you had?"

He laughed, and topped up her mug, then his, although he dared not drink too much. He had to keep his wits about him, all of them.

"The same as you. It's almost empty, and we've been here for..." he pulled out his phone to check the time, "...three hours."

"Still no service?"

He shook his head. "Pippa, I—"

"Jed, unless you possess the ability to predict when an accident will close the main road and force us to take a detour, not to mention when a freak storm will hit, that took everyone by surprise, then I suggest you don't apologize again for our need to spend the night here."

"I should've been better prepared for this."

"Why? If you hadn't been giving me a lift, you'd have driven your rough and ready four-wheel-drive that I need a step ladder to get into. You definitely wouldn't have taken your low-to-the-ground, comfortable, leather-seated sedan. And we'd be back at Kookaburra Crossing sitting in front of a fireplace that worked, drinking wine that wasn't vintage terribilis, and our dinner would be more than a box of chocolates."

"And this is your attempt to make me feel better?"

Her laughter eased some of the tension tightening his shoulders.

"Yes! And a reminder that you didn't kidnap and drag me here. We both agreed that this humble abode..." she gazed pointedly at the rusty bucket they'd placed under the leaking roof, "...was the best option for the night."

Tension of a different kind raced through his body. He'd never been so keen for a night to end, for it never to end.

"As soon as the storm clears, I'll walk out."

"I know. And if my shoes were any less ridiculous, I'd join you. This adventure wasn't what I had in mind, when I chose my outfit this morning."

An outfit, despite now being covered by blankets, he'd never forget. A dress the colour of clear summer skies in a silky looking material, caressed every one of her delicious curves. Teamed with spindly black sandals accentuating smooth legs before they'd disappeared beneath the jagged knee-length hem. He'd ached to run his hands up her legs and keep going. That had only intensified once she'd sat in his car and the hem had hitched up her thighs. He'd held his breath at every one of her wriggles, fidgets, and leg crosses. It was a wonder they hadn't ended up in a ditch.

"Work boots would've spoiled the look," he agreed.

Her eyes flared at his suddenly husky tone, and the space between them vibrated with awareness.

She dropped her gaze to her mug and wrapped her hands around it.

"Mandy would've been horrified if I'd turned up at her wedding wearing any such thing." She raised her eyes and speared him with a look full of remorse. "I hate feeling like some damsel in distress."

He shook his head. "You're no damsel. I've seen you play cards, remember?"

She smiled and his heart flipped in acknowledgement.

"Okay, enough stalling. I'm not going to be deterred from the final round. Then the loser—" she raised her eyebrows, "—pays up."

She stretched a red nailed hand to the chocolates and turned them her way, her mother's signet ring flashing in the candlelight. While Pippa searched the remaining selection, he searched her face. With a minimum of fuss, she picked one, unwrapped it and brought to her lips. He imagined those lips pressed against his.

His blood roared despite the frigid air inside the cottage, and he gripped his chipped mug, amazed it didn't shatter from the force.

CRECD

Pippa's heart skipped a beat, then another as Jed's heated gaze landed on her lips and stayed there. She wanted to run a fingertip along them and imagine it was his. Jamming her eyes closed, she sternly told herself why that would be a bad, bad idea. For years he'd treated her like a kid sister. Why would that change today? She opened her eyes and caught a flash of something in his. Desire, or wishful thinking on her part, a trick of the fading light?

Dropping her hand, she swallowed, and the last traces of chocolate disappeared, calling to mind their game.

"What flavour?" she asked, her voice a croaky sham of its usual timbre.

"Flavour?" He frowned.

"The chocolate..."

He blinked and leant back in his chair.

"Hmmmm... strawberry."

She shook her head. "Orange."

"Best of five?" he asked quickly.

"No chance. I want to claim my prize."

"Okay. Ask me anything." He placed a hand over his heart. "I'm honour bound to answer truthfully." He finished with a wry twist of lips, although sincerity filled his tone.

Inspiration struck, though it took another fortifying sip of the disgusting wine before she could speak. "Have you ever wanted to kiss me?"

Jerking upright, Jed knocked his mug but caught it before spilling anything. "Phillipa!"

"Jeremiah! Answer the question," she added with a hateful tremor. Her bravado wavered and her stomach heaved until she straightened her spine and reminded herself she was made of tougher stuff.

"I kissed you this morning," his voice tight and his usual healthy pallor, testament to the hours he spent outdoors, turning ashen.

She held his gaze. "A peck on my cheek that the sternest matron would approve of isn't what I'm talking about." She felt colour roar to said cheeks and struggled to hold eyes that had turned from navy to black.

Dragging a hand through tawny brown hair, he tousled his permanently tousled style. A look others would spend a fortune trying to manufacture, although she knew he'd never step inside a salon, nor use any product other than shampoo.

"What kind of kiss are you talking about? No! Don't answer that." His hand tunnelled through his hair again. "Your father is my boss. I can't..." Anguish bled through his words, straight into her heart. The fatherless boy and her sonless father had bonded years ago, their deep mutual respect evident and enduring.

"My father has nothing to do with this," she said with passionate insistence. "It's between you and me, and you don't owe me anything – except the truth."

"The truth is, I care about you." Desperation flashed in his eyes.

Disappointment flooded her like burning acid, dousing her hopes. Curling her hands, she clung onto the side of the table to hide their shaking. She wanted to close her eyes, cover her ears, to disappear and pretend she'd never asked the question.

"I didn't mean to embarrass you." Every word felt like it was pushed out through a mouthful of sand.

"Pippa, I..."

He reached out and rested his hands over hers. Heat shot into her veins and for a moment she revelled in his touch, imagining it was desire, not pity, she felt. But it wasn't. Wrenching her hands free, she shot to her feet and headed for the door.

ভগৈৎ

Jed launched upright and blocked her exit. "Hey, stop."

"I don't want your pity. Get away from me." Her voice was

watery, and the sound shattered his already fragile heart. He stepped back but refused to let her pass.

"Pity you?" he parroted. He'd been caught off-guard ever since she'd asked her loaded question. Dread that she'd somehow guessed his deepest desire was now replaced with the gut wrenching need to make her understand that he felt many things for her, but pity wasn't one of them. "No, that's not how I feel."

"Yes, I know, you care about me." She practically spat the words, her face leeched of colour, except for two patches of red, high on her cheeks.

"Yes, I do. I always have." He dragged in a breath and prepared to speak the truth, no matter the consequences. "And I want to kiss you. Really kiss you."

She shook her head. "Don't try and make me feel better about this."

He barked out a humourless laugh. "I think we're both past that."

"Jed..." She closed her eyes and rubbed a palm over her forehead. "The horror on your face told me everything I need to know. I shouldn't have asked, but you know me and my big mouth."

"Surprise, not horror. And I absolutely love everything about you. Especially your big mouth."

Her eyes sprang open, shock and a searing vulnerability radiating from their brown depths.

"But, you should know, this is no game of truth or dare for me," he said.

"I wanted to know. For me. For real." She bit down on her lower lip, and he had to stop himself from reaching for her.

He nodded. "Because you guessed how I feel about you?"

"I have no idea. You've never said anything, or done anything, or given me one clue as to your thoughts."

Queasiness curdled his stomach, which had nothing to do with the wine and everything to do with what was at stake.

"When I realized my feelings for you had changed, I didn't know what to do. Up until that point you'd always been like a kid sister to me, and you know what your father did for my mother and me. I didn't want to betray his trust."

"But I—"

"Let me finish, please. I've waited such a long time to say this." He planted his feet apart needing to get this right, all of it. "You were so young, I decided I'd wait three long torturous years until you were twenty-one. And then you came home from uni and brought your new boyfriend." A sound escaped him, something between a growl and groan at the memory. "You looked happy, really happy for the first time since your mum died. And I realised what you wanted was someone who was polished, professional. Someone who'd know how to order the finest wine in five different languages. Not me, never me. And I was right, because all your boyfriends have been the same. But now." He shook his head. "I can't hide my feelings any longer."

Pippa gasped and he jammed his hands deep into his anorak. Raw and exposed now that he'd said his piece, he'd rather face a charging bull with his feet bound than wait for her response.

"You liked me all the way back then?"

He nodded.

"And that's why you were so formal and distant? Like, literally distant, you were always off in the back paddock whenever I visited home."

He nodded again.

"And five years later, you still like me – like that?"

"Yes," he croaked, all he could manage.

She groaned, and he fisted his hands inside his pockets, dread inching down his spine.

"When I went off to uni I hoped that some distance would kill off my huge crush on you. And I made myself date guys different to you." She shrugged. "But I didn't last with any of them, because they're not you."

The fine hairs at the back of his neck lifted, his eyes never leaving hers.

"What exactly are you saying?"

"I had—" she swallowed and so did he, "—still have, it bad for you."

For a moment he feared he was losing his hearing as a tiny seed of hope planted itself in his heart.

"How bad?"

"Bad bad," she whispered.

Relief charged through him almost bringing him to his knees. Bad bad, her description for anything epic.

He felt a smile form. "Really?"

"Really."

Pippa thought she'd seen every one of Jed's smiles but never one like this, slow and sexy, it zipped straight to her heart, melting it.

"It's my deepest secret," she told him.

"And mine," he said, still smiling.

She huffed out a sigh of relief, hardly believing he felt the same way about her.

Pippa stepped forward as the generous dimensions of his chest and shoulders filled her horizon. Reaching out, he gently looped one of her curls around his fingers.

"So soft," he said with reverence.

Vibrating with an aching desperate need, she captured his strong capable hands and linked them with hers. Her body quivered, tightened.

"I'll give you everything, Pippa, from these calloused hands, to the very last breath in my body. If you want it, it's yours, all of it. And if that means moving to the city to be with you, then that's what I'll do," he said, low and impassioned, his eyes more intense than she'd ever seen them.

She blinked back a tear.

"You'd leave here, for me?" Incredulous, she stared at him. How could this amazing man amaze her any more than he did?

"For you, yes. You see I've got it bad bad, for you."

Pure joy filled her heart, her laugh.

"Don't leave. I want to come home, to be here with you. For good."

His eyes glowed. Excitement simmered between them.

"We can discuss the details later. I think we've waited long enough for this, don't you?"

He didn't wait for her answer, instead he lowered his head and she reached up to meet his lips in a kiss that she felt to her very soul. His real kiss. It tasted of chocolate, and home, and forever.

13
BITTER SWEET
VALERIE MILLER

Mallory kicked the engine over. Nothing.

"Damn."

She stormed out and slammed the door.

Just what she needed. As if she did not have enough problems in her life right now. With no job, a wedding that should have been hers and a traitor for a best friend. The only good thing about it was being able to escape from it all to care for Gran.

The worry over her Gran's broken leg returned, and then panic settled in — Gran's chocolates!

A kookaburra cackled nearby. Mallory checked her phone. Late. She needed to get a move on. The country fair opened to the public today and the stall needed to be set up.

She spied the bike tucked away at the side of the garage. The basket was perfect to put Gran's containers in.

The old tourist road made the ride easier, and the exercise swept her frustration away. She imagined being in a French movie — cycling along in her straw hat and crisp linen shirt. Above, wispy clouds peppered a powder blue sky and early butterflies flirted around wildflowers.

A perfect spring morning.

Until the front wheel came loose. Mallory lost her balance and careened into the ditch.

Great! She brushed the dirt off her shirt and swallowed hard to stop the tears.

"Are you okay?"

Mallory turned to see Ellis Taylor looking down at her. His creased forehead matched the concern in his voice.

He still looked good, in a rugged kind of way, with his stubble and tousled hair. She had not seen him since moving away from Birchwood Falls.

"Yes." She stood up and flinched at the pain. "No."

He strode down. "You're bleeding."

"Yep. When I do something, I do it spectacularly."

Ellis bobbed down and inspected the wounds. Did he recognise her? Why would he? Seniors never took any notice of the younger grades. He had been in year eleven when she had started high school.

"This needs dressing. I've got a first aid kit in the ute. Can you walk?" He placed his hand on her elbow.

"I think so." She limped over and tried to lift the bike up. "I've made a mess of my Gran's bike."

"I've got it." He rushed over.

"Be careful of the chocolates."

"Chocolates?"

"They're Gran's. She makes them. I'm taking them to the fair and running the stall this weekend. She's broken her leg."

Mallory took the containers from Ellis and inspected them, "Thank goodness for Tupperware and jockey straps."

Ellis stood there. Following her every move until he clicked his fingers and laughed.

"Mallory McQueen!"

"Yep."

"I haven't seen you—"

"Since I was a spindly, freckled face teenager?" She scuttled out a laugh. Mallory pointed at the bike. "And I'm still clumsy," she joked, trying to make light of her growing embarrassment. She followed Ellis' quick glance and gasped. Her shirt gaped open, exposing her plain white bra. She fumbled with the buttons.

Thank goodness Ellis averted his eyes and focused on collecting her scattered belongings.

"You better check it's all there." He handed over her purse and phone.

She tsked at the cracked screen.

"Sorry about your phone."

Mallory shrugged to hide her disappointment.

"Just a phone, right."

"Let me help you to the ute."

"Thanks."

Mallory nursed her shattered pride and watched Ellis take control — the calm agile way he sauntered down the ditch, picked up the bike and carried it back to the road.

She checked herself in the rear-view mirror and pulled out a couple of dry leaves from her hair. *What a mess*. Behind, Ellis came into view as he placed her bike in the ute's tray. Mallory adjusted her gaze and watched him strap the bike down and grab the first aid kit.

"This might sting."

Mallory did not feel a thing. Ellis dressed her wounds with care. His hands were tanned and calloused, yet his gentleness surprised her. To steady her knee, he placed his broad hand behind her calf. The heat shot up her leg, straight into the pit of her stomach. Mallory studied Ellis as he focused on her injuries. She imagined brushing his wavy hair out of his eyes.

He stopped dressing the second knee and looked up at her. Her reflection spilled into his pale blue eyes. Embarrassed by her thoughts, Mallory jerked her head away, hitting the side of the door frame.

"Did I hurt you?" he said, a small crease formed above his nose.

"No. Yes. I mean, no." The words bumbled out of her.

Ellis grinned and packed up the first aid kit.

"What have you been up to?" Mallory asked, covering up her awkwardness and ignoring the humming in her heart.

"Working the dairy with Dad and Gavin."

"Do you still have the best cows in the district?"

"Yep. Some new prize winners too. You know that's why your Gran's got the best winning chocolate. She uses our milk." He stood up and winked at Mallory.

"Oh, is that right?"

She enjoyed his playfulness and started to relax a little.

"You know, we're sharing the same stall."

Mallory bit her lip. She took in a few slow breaths to settle her thumping heart. She enjoyed this attention.

"That will be delightful." Mallory cringed at the comment. What did she just say?

Ellis chuckled as he handed her the Tupperware containers. She sunk down into the seat and winced. Ellis must think she was a right twit.

She caught the bemused look on his face. He did!

Ellis shook his head, his eyes filled with laughter as he shut the car door. He smiled to himself as he walked across the front of the ute to the driver's side.

"Did I say something funny?" she asked when he slid into the driver's seat.

He looked at her. "Delightful?" He started the engine, "Sounds like we're in an Austen novel."

Mallory turned with surprise.

"Austen novel? I'm shocked you even know what an Austen novel is?"

"Oh, I know plenty." He grinned.

Was he making fun of her? It was year seven all over again, and Ellis was the confident senior who knew it all.

Mallory decided to keep quiet. Every time she opened her mouth, she dug herself deeper into the-what-a-ninny-universe. Instead, she focused on the farmlands that flashed past as they drove towards Wilson's property, where the Fair was held each year.

It was the perfect place.

Nestled in a valley, surrounded by rolling blue-green eucalyptus forest. The Wilson's also owned an enormous barn, the ideal venue for the Country Fair dance.

It was the highpoint of the weekend. The entire district came together. But Mallory was not going. It would be like a school reunion, but much worse. Everyone already wanted to know everyone's business. Why should Mallory give them any more fodder?

Besides, she had no more emotional energy to deal with their questions — What are you doing? Are you seeing someone? Knowing each time, she responded with 'nothing' or 'nobody', another piece of her self-esteem would be stripped away.

She had already instructed Gran not to tell anyone about her breakup or the wedding.

Mallory had planned to stay home watching TV with Gran instead.

But Gran went and hired a wheelchair just for the occasion.

"It's bad enough I won't be able to sell my own chocolates. It's the biggest social event of Birchwood Falls, and I'm not missing it," she'd said.

Who was Mallory to argue with her Gran? She lived alone and deserved some social excitement in her life.

"Have you got a hot date?"

"Don't be ridiculous." Gran shook the morning paper at her.

Mallory leaned over, scoffed down some toast and waved the remaining half as a lady's fan, playing the coy southern belle.

"I declare. Where is my gentleman caller?"

"Very funny." Gran gave her a pointed look and waved her out the door. "Scoot. That stall won't set itself up."

The ute hit a pothole and pulled Mallory out of her thoughts. No car.

"Shoot!"

"Are you in pain?" Ellis asked. The concern in his voice melted Mallory into the worn vinyl seat.

"No. I have to drive Gran to the dance tonight, but my car has a flat battery. That's why you found me tangled up in a busted bike and looking like a dishevelled street cat."

"Street cat? More like Bridget Jones."

"Wow, you really know your chick-lit."

"There's a lot about me you don't know." He kept his eyes straight ahead. "None of this farm-boy-stereotyping thank you."

"I wouldn't dream of it."

She stole quick glances at Ellis. He did have a great sense of humour. At school he always laughed and joked with his friends. And the senior girls always flocked around him. Why wouldn't they? He always had a bewitching smile. Still did. What would it be like to kiss him? She pictured him grabbing and tickling her — the two of them falling onto the ground in a romantic embrace.

"What are you going to do?"

Caught out, Mallory felt her face explode with heat and jerked around so fast she nearly dropped the chocolates off her lap.

"Sorry?"

"About getting your Gran to the dance," said Ellis.

Mallory pulled her knees up, creating a barrier to stop the chocolates slipping onto the floor. "I'll get an Uber home, then call the NRMA."

"Uber? Not likely here. And the NRMA will take hours." Ellis turned into the Wilson's property. His hands handled the wheel with ease.

"Oh?"

Ellis swung the ute into a vacant spot and stopped. He turned to Mallory and smiled. "Would you like me to drive you back at the end of the day?"

"That would be great. If it's no trouble."

"Not at all. My carriage awaits."

"And the hits keep coming," she said.

"Yes, they do." He laughed.

Ellis put her at ease. She missed being with someone like this. No! Mallory pushed the thought away. She was not going to succumb to some fly-by-night crush because she was alone and vulnerable. No. No. No, she kept repeating to herself.

⦂⦂⦂

Mallory trundled into the living room.

"Oh, my goodness, what happened to you?"

Gran struggled to get up on her crutches.

"Don't get up." She rushed over to Gran. "It's just the Betadine that makes it look bad. I had a little accident."

"Mallory, you haven't changed. Always getting banged up."

"Yep, in more ways than you know." She gave Gran a hug. "You're dressed early."

"I hope you don't mind, but Ruth's offered to take me for a bite to eat, then to the dance. I think that woman is trying to get her mitts onto my chocolate recipe."

"I don't blame her. I sold all your chocolates. People kept coming back for more."

"Good. And tomorrow, the visitors will return. It'll bring them back to the Fair. You'll have order forms so they can buy them online."

"Gran, you're a real entrepreneur."

"I'm not just a pretty face." She winked. "Anyway, you're off the hook. You can stay home, like you wanted."

"Oh? Okay."

Mallory tried to hide her disappointment. Although she had not wanted to go to the dance, spending the day with Ellis warmed her up about going.

"Yoo-hoo." Ruth stepped in from the kitchen. "Hello, Mallory. Was that young Ellis, I saw you with at the Fair?"

Mallory caught Gran's cocked eyebrow.

"Yep. We shared the same stall."

Gran looked thrilled. Had it not been for Gran's broken leg, Mallory would have believed she'd devised the whole day. All of it. Sabotaging her car, the front bike tyre, Ellis on the country road instead of the highway. Come to think of it, she was lucky he had taken the tourist route. Otherwise, she would still be in that ditch. Everyone took the highway.

"They turned up together." Ruth fussed around Gran.

Man, that woman could gossip. Mallory shot her a look.

"Did they now?" Gran smiled.

Great.

That was all Mallory needed right now. For the human bush telegram, a.k.a, Ruth Peterson, to tell everyone she and Ellis were a potential item. Or worse still, flirtatious. How mortifying! Nearly as mortifying as telling people your boyfriend cheated on you with your best friend, knocked her up, then married her in a lavish wedding that put the Kardashians to shame.

She would not be able to show her face in Birchwood Falls again. Humiliated in her hometown, as well as in the city.

"We're just friends," Mallory said, flicking the comment away.

"Didn't look like it to me," Ruth said as she helped Gran into the wheelchair.

"Don't you have dinner reservations?" said Mallory. She opened the door to hustle them out. "Have a great time." She kissed Gran on the cheek. "You look gorgeous. Do you need an umbrella?"

"Why? There's not a cloud about." Gran looked up. Dusk now settled across the quiet valley.

"To beat the fellas off." Mallory smiled.

"Stop being cheeky," said Gran.

Ruth fussed over Gran, who returned an annoyed swat. Chuckles escaped from both of them. They really were the best of friends. She pressed her lips and smiled wistfully. She wished for just half the companionship that Gran and Ruth enjoyed. Now, thanks to Ruth, she would soon to be the laughing-stock in town.

Mallory sighed and waited until they were gone. She shut the front door and leaned against it. The events of the day filtered in and out of her mind. Ellis' smile dominated.

She shook her head. Come on, get a grip. Someone like Ellis would never be interested in her. He was a catch. Good looking farmers were in hot demand now, thanks to reality TV. The women flirted and lash batted at him all day – every single one of them. Nope, she was the comic relief. A prize klutz.

They did have fun. His stories were hilarious, and he spoke to her in a way that made her feel special. He asked about her life in the city and what she liked doing.

Mallory worked hard to keep her emotions in check. He was being friendly because they shared the stall. That's all. It made the time go by faster, and Ellis was brought up right — to be polite.

⊂≋⊃

Mallory treated herself. She washed her hair, put on a face mask, and moisturised her entire body. She even used a hairdryer. Her grazed knees and elbow still looked raw, but she covered them up with band-aids — out of sight, out of mind. No wounds and no reminder of being found sprawled in a ditch.

The doorbell rang.

Finally. She was starving.

She opened the door. Ellis stood there, holding her Chinese takeaway.

"Come on. Don't tell me you deliver Chinese food on the side?"

"Maybe?"

He held up a bottle of wine.

Man, that smile. Her skin tingled under her cotton robe.

"Really? I thought milking cows kept you busy. Don't you guys get up at six am?"

"Actually, it's four am. Can I come in?"

"Sure." Mallory adjusted her bathrobe and stepped back. Her bare heel clipped the hall runner, and she stumbled. Ellis reached over and grabbed her, pulling her into him. He smelt great. A spicy woody scent enveloped her. She moved out from under his gaze and tucked strands of hair behind her ears.

"Why aren't you at the dance?" he said.

"Not something I was in the mood for."

"I see." He looked around the living room, then sat down.

"Make yourself at home." Mallory tried to be sarcastic but felt the smile sneak up.

"Don't mind if I do."

"Are you always so..." she wanted to say 'gorgeous, loveable, adorable', but she caught the thought and wrestled it into submission.

"So...?" Ellis' eyes locked onto hers.

"Confident. No. Smug."

Mallory sat opposite him and crossed her legs. She winced as her knee bent and pulled at the wound.

"Careful." Ellis smiled. "We don't want you any more damaged than you already are."

Was he flirting? A coy awkwardness gripped her. Ellis Taylor pushed through the loneliness in her heart and pulverised it with attentive humour.

Mallory knew deep down, there was an attraction. Ellis' concern. His playfulness in the car. The genuine way he looked straight at her when he smiled and the light-hearted teasing while they worked on their stalls together.

They sat there. Ellis quite comfortable. He stared straight at her. Mallory returned a look, then glanced away.

"Would you like some wine?" they both chimed in together, then erupted into laughter.

"Yes," they both said together again, forcing them to laugh louder.

Mallory got up and grabbed a couple of glasses from the kitchen.

She felt Ellis behind her and turned. He stood there; his eyes burned into her. Mallory took in some staggered breaths.

"Wine?"

She held up the glasses.

Ellis moved towards her and took each glass out of her hands. He kept his eyes on her and placed them on the bench.

"I gather no," Mallory whispered.

Ellis shook his head. He moved a wayward strand of her hair and twirled it between his fingers before he tucked it behind her ear.

"Ellis…"

Ellis placed his finger on her lips, then lifted her chin up, leaned in and kissed her.

Mallory slowed her breathing down. She stopped thinking, and she stopped worrying.

His kiss was gentle.

She sidestepped her nerves and kissed him back.

Ellis, sensing her acceptance, kissed her, this time with all the passion he felt. The kiss freed Mallory, and she gave herself over to him.

When they pulled apart. Ellis grinned at her.

"Well, that's one heck of a way of delivering Chinese," Mallory whispered.

"I've wanted to kiss you all day." He stroked her cheek.

"Me too." She moved into his arms. She felt safe and wanted.

"Hey." She looked up at him. "Why aren't *you* at the dance?"

"I ran into Ruth and your Gran at *The Green Jade*."

"Ruth!"

"Yep. She sure likes to talk," Ellis winked. "A lot."

14
OPERATION CHOCOLATE DROP

GEORGIA MOORE

The front door is wide open. I grasp my satchel strap, double-checking the number on the door.

"Hello?" I call.

No reply.

I edge inside, my heels loud on the tiled floor, and am hit with an overpowering scent of chocolate. I wrinkle my nose, feeling like I've stepped into Willy Wonka's factory.

There's no sign of the owner, so I walk through the entryway and emerge in a kitchen-living-dining-entertainment room. The space feels cramped. Every surface – from the kitchen island to the coffee table – is covered in trays holding tiny chocolates. The total number must be astronomical if they've spilled into here from the chocolate making facility next door. I'll have to find out the exact figure for my article.

I pull my notebook from my bag and write the question down. This is my first lifestyle article for the *Blue Valley Daily*, something I've been working towards for two years. I wish I had more time to prepare but I'm not going to waste this last-minute opportunity to prove myself.

"Hello? Matthew?" I call again.

"Coming!"

The holler sounds from down the hall. I turn, freezing when a man emerges from one of the doors dragging a t-shirt over a well-defined chest smattered with blond hair.

I snap my jaw shut as heat spreads over my cheeks.

That never happened at any of my interviews for the real estate section. It hasn't happened in a while for me, period. Being alone in a house with an attractive man, that is. Not since I dumped Colin.

But now isn't the time to be thinking about that as the man walks over and holds out a hand. I shake it, getting lost in his warm brown eyes.

"Sorry about that." He has a voice warm as the sun and a smile that presses dimples into his cheeks. "Thought I'd have time for a quick shower but must've misjudged."

"It's fine." It comes out breathy, so I clear my throat and repeat it.

"Matthew Covings. Call me Matt."

"Tanya Blake."

"Welcome, Tanya. Can I get you anything? Tea? Coffee? Hot chocolate?"

"Just water, thanks."

He heads into the kitchen area and grabs two glasses from a cupboard, filling them at the sink. I follow him over, trying to refocus on the job. With his broad shoulders and blond hair, Matt is exactly my type, but I'm on the clock and this article is a big opportunity for me.

"Find the place okay?" he asks, passing me a glass.

"No troubles."

"Good." The dimpled smile returns, and I actually feel a fluttering of butterfly wings in my stomach.

I turn and survey the room. Even the dining chairs haven't escaped the abundance of chocolates. "Maybe we should do the interview outside. It looks... busy here."

Matt laughs, a big belly laugh with no restraint. "You can say 'pigsty'. Actually," he backtracks, "I grew up on a farm. That was much more organised than this."

"And what is *this*?" I nod to the chocolates, taking the opening to start the interview. I got the run-down from my boss, Heather, but it's always good to hear it from the source.

"Operation Chocolate Drop," Matt announces with a sweep of his arm. "I make hand-crafted chocolates for everyone in town, which is just under one thousand five hundred this year. My biggest yet."

My eyes widen thinking about how much effort Matt must put into the project. Certainly more than Colin put into our relationship. He didn't even get me chocolates on Valentine's Day.

I take a breath and shove thoughts of Colin away, annoyed I've been distracted yet again from what could be the most important interview of my career to date. "So, what made you start Operation Chocolate Drop?"

"Well..."

⊂Ƨ∞⊃

We end up sitting outside around a wrought-iron table so small our knees keep knocking, sending littles *zings* up my leg which increase in frequency the further into the interview we get, as my admiration for Matt grows.

"I think we're done," I say after forty minutes, having asked everything on my list. "Just the photos now."

"Should I change?"

"You're great."

Matt raises his eyebrows, but it's with total sincerity that he says, "I think you're great, too."

Feeling my cheeks warm, I busy myself readying the camera. "I meant the clothes you're in are fine."

"Where do you want me?"

The question prompts a litany of inappropriate thoughts and I'm thankful my loose hair shields my cheeks. "Kitchen, please."

I give him a head start while I reset my brain to professional mode. It evaporates when we begin shooting. Matt is relaxed in front of the camera, his big smile and beautiful eyes directed right at me. We take plenty of photos around the kitchen, then in his backyard where he starts messing around, juggling chocolates.

My stomach hurts from laughing by the time I declare I've taken enough.

"Can I see?" Matt asks.

"Sure."

He stands behind me, close enough I can feel his body heat. I hope he doesn't notice my shaking hands.

"Did you train as a photographer?" he asks as we look.

I shake my head. "But we all get a crash-course at the *Daily*, in case our photographer isn't available."

"You have a great eye for it then."

I turn to look at him. We're standing close for two people who only met an hour ago. I don't mind at all, especially when Matt's gaze drops to my lips and my stomach butterflies quiver.

He backs away a second later and I'm second-guessing what I saw when my phone rings.

"Hey, Heather," I answer.

"Tanya. Where are you?"

No pleasantries. Uh-oh. My heart rate kicks up a notch. I hope it's just continued stress from Louise's food poisoning.

"Just finished interviewing Matthew."

"Fantastic. Look, the deadlines have been reshuffled. Your piece is due 4pm today."

My stomach gets heavy. "What? That's..." I check my watch. "Three hours away!"

"I know. I'm sorry. But marketing's already shifted the advertising tie-in with the chocolate boxes."

My heart pounds so hard I can hear my pulse. My gaze bounces around before I spy Matt in his kitchen. He looks up a second later and smiles at me, then winks before throwing a chocolate up in the air and catching it in his mouth.

My laugh's a little strangled, but it's there and it takes the edge off my panic. If Matt can handmake hundreds of chocolates in a few days, I can write this article in a few hours.

I take a deep breath. "I'll get it to you."

Pressure builds behind my eyes, but this article is important for my career. I need to come up with a plan of attack. I open my notebook and draw a rough table, breaking my time into smaller chunks.

"Everything all right?" Matt steps outside, frowning.

"The article is due today. But it'll be fine. I don't have time to type up my notes or properly listen back to anything. So, not ideal, but if I get it down quick it should be fine. So. Okay. Half an hour drive to the office." I scribble it onto my table. "Then first draft done by, say, two-thirty. Then fact-checking, which—"

"Write it here."

I startle. "Pardon?"

"Why don't you write it here? It'll give you that extra half-hour and I can answer questions as they come up."

I swallow my immediate reaction to turn down his offer. When I was with Colin, offers like this were never sincere and often came paired with a sense of me owing him if I did accept them.

After interviewing him, I know Matt won't be like that. "Thank you."

I duck out to my car for my laptop and when I return, Matt has cleared a space on the dining table. He's nowhere to be seen, but a post-it note on the table proclaims, 'You can do it!'. I settle into the space with a smile and get to work.

C33&D

It takes until my third draft to realise my article is lacking something. Heart. I curse at the obvious omission. That's the part I love about real-life stories and I'm embarrassed I almost missed it.

"Why today?" I throw out the question but there's no reply.

I shift my focus from my laptop to look for Matt, noticing the stiffness in my neck as I do. "Matt?"

"Yeah?"

He pops out of a doorway in his hall, fully dressed this time. I swallow a sigh. Some shirtlessness would have been a nice reprieve.

"Why do the drop now?"

"What do you mean?" Matt walks into the kitchen and pulls out a wooden chopping board.

"Why not Valentine's Day or something?"

"February is too hot to be working with this much chocolate," Matt teases, opening his fridge and arranging a selection of food on the board.

My stomach rumbles and I realise I've missed lunch. "Why a random day that's different every year, then?"

Matt stills and my leg ceases bouncing. With his back to me, I can't see his expression, but his shoulders are noticeably stiff.

"I don't do it on Valentine's because I think any day can be special if you want it to be," he eventually says, turning to lean against the kitchen counter. "We should be celebrating and expressing love every day, not waiting until Valentine's or New Year's or a birthday."

"Sounds like there's a story there. What happened?" The corners of his mouth turn down and my heart sinks. "Sorry. My journalist side took over. You don't have to answer. I don't need it for the article."

Before I can return to my work his gaze hooks onto mine and I freeze. I'm certain I'm seeing the Matt beneath the carefree exterior.

"You're right," he says. "There's a story."

He picks up his board of food and carries it to the dining table, placing it between us before sitting down.

His gaze lingers over my shoulder as he speaks.

"I'd been seeing someone for a few years and things were going well, so well I was going to propose. I put all my focus and free time toward planning this big Valentine's Day proposal. Missing dinners with her to organise it, lying about an out-of-town event so I could look at rings. I was looking so much into the future I didn't realise I was neglecting her in the present. She broke things off a few weeks before Valentine's. Said some stuff that was hard to hear. I tried to explain the situation but she'd made her decision."

My heart clenches. "I'm sorry."

"You don't have to be. But thanks." He gives me a wry smile. "Took me a while to actually accept what she accused me of. Now I make sure to cherish all my relationships every day, romantic or otherwise."

Perhaps I shouldn't, but it's easy to imagine being cherished by Matt. Even now, after he's just shared the ugly parts of his story.

He pushes the board of food closer to me and says, "For you."

There's a fluttering in my stomach as I dunk a cracker into some dip. I didn't say a thing about being hungry, but he anticipated my need anyway.

"And do you have a romantic relationship currently?" I'm asking before I've thought it through.

I shove the cracker in my mouth to stop more embarrassing questions. I could blame the hunger, the stress of the deadline, or the impending headache, but I know they're lies. I like Matt and I'm drawn to him like I haven't been to anyone since Colin. I want to know more about him and it's completely personal.

He raises his eyebrows. "Is this the journalistic side coming out again?"

I groan. "Please ignore that question." I turn my attention to my laptop for good measure and start to type, though it's total gibberish.

"Alright." He laughs lightly, pushing back from the table, leaving the food with me. "The answer's no, by the way."

Relief floods me, but the unprofessional interlude is a reminder I need to get back to work. I only have forty minutes left to incorporate the new information and get the article done to a standard that's not merely good enough to print, but *great* enough to impress Heather so I'll get the chance to write lifestyle articles again.

I hurriedly eat another few crackers, delete the gibberish, then knuckle down.

CRTO

With fourteen minutes to spare, I ask Matt to read my final version.

He unearths a pair of thin wire-rimmed glasses from a drawer in his kitchen. They take his looks from boy-next-door to millennial entrepreneur. My exhausted brain has no willpower to pull my gaze off him while he sits at the dining table and reads.

When he's done, he hooks the glasses into the V of his t-shirt. "You've spelled my name wrong."

"What?" I grab for my laptop, but Matt traps my hands on the table.

"Sorry. That was my attempt at a joke. It's good. The article is great."

Since I leaned across the table for my laptop, our faces are now close enough I can see faint freckles on his nose and cheeks. I wonder if they get darker in summer and get a sad pang in my chest when I realise I'll never know.

"You looked like you could use a laugh," he apologises again. "I've never seen someone so focussed on work before. It was... You're inspiring. Honestly."

The butterflies flutter.

Matt's hands still cover mine. They're warm and heavy and make me think he'd be a great hugger. "You're pretty inspiring too," I tell him. Our gaze holds and, like earlier, I imagine Matt's focus drops to my lips. I must be exhausted.

"I need to do a final read and send this."

"Right. Of course." Matt pushes his chair back from the table and a gut impulse has me reaching out to grab his wrist.

His eyes widen and I feel his pulse race beneath my fingertips. I'm definitely not imaging that, but I try not to ascribe any meaning to it beyond surprise.

"Thank you," I say with all the sincerity I feel.

C3&80

I hit send right on deadline.

I exhale roughly and slump onto the table for a moment, letting my body go limp before standing up and lifting my arms above my head. I shut my eyes, breathing slowly in and out, and stretch to the side, ignoring the sound of Matt dropping something in the kitchen.

My neck will definitely be sore tomorrow, but it's done. I know with another few days I could have turned in something better, but considering all the handicaps I was working with, I'm proud of my article. Hopefully, Heather feels similarly. I'll have to set up a meeting with her later this week to talk about it.

I drop my arms, noticing a packet of Panadol and a glass of

water have appeared on the table. This is the second – third, fourth? I've lost count – act of unprompted thoughtfulness from Matt and it excites the butterflies inside me.

I swallow two Panadol, then, with the board of food still on the table, I eat some more of the crackers and dip. It's a stalling tactic. Now that I've sent the article, I have no reason to linger in Matt's house aside from my own personal curiosity and attraction.

Packing up is too quick and suddenly I'm in his entryway with my stomach heavy inside me. Knowing I'll never see Matt again sours my triumph at submitting the article.

"It's been wonderful, Matt. The interview and the... Anyway. Thanks."

"Don't mention it."

Even though I've stared so much today, I let myself take a lingering look at him.

"Oh," Matt exclaims suddenly, placing a hand on my arm like I was in danger of walking out the door. My skin buzzes.

"I almost forgot." Matt jogs down the corridor and returns seconds later with a small white box.

"What's this?" Our fingers graze as I take it, renewing the buzzing of my skin. I open it to see four beautiful chocolates. One has my name piped onto it.

My throat dries up and I find myself throwing my arms around Matt. I'm shocked at myself but there's no time for panic because Matt doesn't hesitate to lift his arms and wrap them around me, holding me tightly.

Matt's philosophy about not putting off celebrating or expressing your feelings must have gotten into my head. It's the only logical explanation for why I've got my arms around his solid, warm body. Of course, there are plenty of illogical, attraction-based reasons too.

Hugging him is as wonderful as I thought it would be. My stomach lightens as I breathe in, smelling chocolate and a bergamot-scented aftershave. There's something about Matt I like, *several* somethings, and not all physical. His smile is beautiful, and his eyes are honest, but he's also selfless and quick to offer help without me having to ask for it.

"What was that for?" he asks, laughing, when I pull back.

He's probably not expecting a serious answer, but he's been earnest with me all day and I want to meet his sincerity. Besides, thinking about Matt's philosophy on relationships has made me realise that never seeing him again isn't my only option.

"Because I wanted to."

His smile fades slowly. Have I overstepped? I can't guess what he's feeling but I think I see surprise, maybe a little awe too.

"You're off the clock, right?"

It's not the question I was expecting. "Yes."

"Do you want to stay for dinner? I'd love to spend more time with you."

The butterflies take flight inside me, and my smile hurts my cheeks. "I'd love to stay for dinner."

His smile comes out like sunshine after a storm, and I decide that I'm a convert to his philosophy on relationships.

15
SWEET TOOTH

KRISTIN SILK

"**N**ige, it's an emergency." Rosie's voice is laced with desperation, a true addict. Her drug of choice is anything sweet, especially chocolate. Her eyes widen, pleading. "Need chocolate." In the eleven months she's been my housemate, I've heard this phrase more times than I care to remember.

"An emergency?" I raise my eyebrows.

"PMT without chocolate is an emergency." One look into those big brown eyes and I know it's only a matter of time before I crack, walk three blocks to the nearest shop, and return with chocolate.

Rosie swings her legs as she sits on the kitchen bench. Her hair, dyed a violent shade of red, is piled on top of her head in a messy bun. I lean against the counter next to her and rummage in my pocket. "It's not chocolate, but I think I've got something." I pull the sweet out and hand it to her.

Her eyes narrow. "Is this one of those sugar free lollies?"

I nod.

She frowns at the lolly. "Damn you, Satan."

"I live to kill joy."

She unwraps it and pops it into her mouth. "Who even bothers to make sugar free lollies? Sugar is the whole point of lollies."

Rosie is a dentist's nightmare, a chocoholic who doesn't floss and can't remember the last time she had a dental check.

The look on her face as she moves the sweet around her mouth, tells me it's a poor chocolate substitute. "No wonder that kid ran away from you screaming."

"I didn't even offer him a lolly. He just took one look at my face and started crying."

Rosie laughs, her hand on my arm in an easy sign of affection, one that says I'm no threat to her equilibrium whatsoever because I am firmly in the friendzone. My whole body twitches to life at the casual touch. I shut it down. Pretend its fine she thinks of me as a platonic friend, despite the slow, sinking feeling in my gut.

"Maybe you need an image makeover. Some kind of sexy alter ego. Like the Cavity Avenger. Tooth Man. The Funky Flosser."

I chuckle at her stupid names, wishing, not for the first time, that I had a job that was sexy or swoon worthy – a firefighter, rock star or CEO. But no, I'm a dentist. Fighting cavities isn't sexy in anyone's language.

"Would you floss if I offered you chocolate?"

"Nige." An incidental brush against my arm that goes straight to my groin. "You know I would do literally anything for chocolate."

Outrageous statement. "I'll teach you how to floss properly. Dental hygiene is important."

She bites back a grin. "Do you lie awake at night worrying about my dental hygiene?"

"Actually, yes."

Her eyes widen. "Seriously?"

"Yes."

"Like, for real?"

I nod stiffly, cheeks heating.

"Oh my God, that's adorable." Rosie watches me for a long moment. "Okay, you can teach me how to floss. But only if you let me teach *you* how to floss."

She jumps off the kitchen bench and starts moving her hips and arms. I frown. Turns out flossing is some dance move all the kids are into.

"Uh. Okay. But my kind of flossing first."

Rosie follows me into the bathroom. I pull out the dental floss and demonstrate. She follows my lead. Flossing your teeth with someone is not a sexy activity but being in the small room with her so close has my pulse pounding in my ears.

She applies herself to the task with adorable earnestness, her brow crinkling in concentration.

When we finish, Rosie smiles at me in the mirror. "You were right. My teeth feel so clean."

I give her a triumphant grin, which fades at the gleam in her eyes. She grabs my hand, pulling me into the lounge room. "My kind of flossing now."

Uh oh. What have I agreed to? Rosie is a singer in a band, and therefore, has rhythm.

I, on the other hand, am the most uncoordinated man on the planet.

Rosie demonstrates, moving her hips and arms from side to side. My attempts to follow her example have her doubling over with laughter. I don't even care that it's at my expense. I laugh too. There's no one else in the world for whom I would endure this kind of embarrassment. But for Rosie, I would do anything.

She persists in trying to teach me, even though I'm hopeless. She has more chance of teaching a cactus to floss than this unco dentist.

"That's it! You're getting it." I'm sure she's just being kind, but she's flossing with me, putting a hand on my hip every now and then to adjust my movements. She's smiling up at me, and I'm smiling at her, and it feels like a helium balloon is trying to force its way out of my chest.

If chocolate is Rosie's weakness, my weakness is definitely Rosie.

CЯ8Ɔ

I'm without a doubt the most awkward man in the pub, standing alone at a table wearing a neatly ironed shirt tucked into my best dress jeans. Rosie's band, Icarus Burns, is about to come on.

The hip crowd with their tattoos, piercings and ripped jeans languish against the bar with studied indifference while I stand stiffly, sipping my beer, wishing there were a cure for social anxiety. The sharp tang of alcohol hits my nostrils.

Then Rosie strides onto the stage and my heart – stops. Her hair is wild flame flowing over her shoulders. She wears a sheer red dress over black leggings and a black top. Black boots.

There's a sharp edge to her. This is Stage Rosie. Performing Rosie. She exudes confidence and raw sexuality. As the lead singer, she commands the stage.

Then she starts to sing, and it's like spring blooming inside me after a cold, dark winter. Her deep, throaty, powerful voice hits me right in the chest, and other, less noble places. Something low and hungry uncurls inside me and throbs painfully.

The first song is a loud, thrashy number, about being brave enough to fly into the sun, even if you get burned. As a cautious, list-making man, that idea scares the hell out of me, but Rosie's killing it on stage. She's electric, cradling the microphone like a lover. She's a musical enchantress, weaving her spell over the audience until every gaze in the room is on those full, sexy lips as she sings about Icarus burning.

I don't know how she does it, creates all these *feelings* in me, in a way no one else does. I want her so much it hurts. Not just Stage Rosie, though Stage Rosie is sexy beyond belief. But all the Rosies. Chocoholic Rosie. Funny Rosie. The Rosie that cried at the mean cat in *Babe*.

I sip my beer and my hand trembles. The emotion inside me swells until I can hardly swallow past the lump in my throat. Thank Christ it's dark in here.

I sigh inwardly. It's hopeless. Rosie is sexy, bold, and gorgeous. A wild brumby, running free with the wind in her hair. I'm an awkwardly shy dentist. An animal bred in captivity, pacing its cage. I'm Clark Kent without the cool, superhero alias.

Even knowing this, I crave her with an intensity that's almost unbearable. If she goes home with another guy it will kill me.

I'm painfully aware that Rosie has a type, and I'm not it. Several of them lurk in the audience. Bad boy wannabe rock stars with egos the size of small planets. Uber cool and casually heartless.

Like Dylan, Rosie's ex, who was such a consummate liar that he lied about lying. The way that jerk eroded Rosie's confidence and made her feel small, made me want to give him a root canal without anaesthetic.

My hand tightens on my glass. I take a steadying breath and deliberately try to relax it. If Rosie were mine, I wouldn't let her doubt her worth for a single second.

She moves into a quieter song now, letting the audience see everything she feels and making us feel it too. I'm grateful for the chance to watch her without having to maintain the charade of casual friendship. It's getting harder and harder to pretend, when underneath I'm burning for her, churning with a volcano of need.

If only I was someone else – Superman instead of Clark Kent. Rosie's jokes about my dentist alter ego filter into my mind, and the idea hits me like a thunderbolt. What if there was a way to show her how I feel without her knowing it was me? And there, in the dark, crowded pub, Secret Nigel is born.

CS80

I've been crawling with a strange mix of nerves and excitement all day. At the sight of the flowers on the kitchen bench, I silently congratulate myself. Bright red roses, the colour of Rosie's hair, are interspersed with chocolate love hearts wrapped in red foil, attached to stalks like flowers. I raise my eyebrows at her in fake surprise. "Yours?"

She grins and my heart flips over. She rushes to show me the card, her arm brushing mine as she looks over my shoulder while I read it. Of course, I already know what it says: *Dear Rosie, I greatly admire you. Love, SN.*

"Whose SN?" Secret Nigel is sexy and swoon worthy, brave enough to tell the woman he loves how he feels about her. Real Nigel? Not so much.

"I have no idea." Her eyes, the colour of melted chocolate, widen.

I fall into them. Force a casual smile. "You have an admirer."

Her cheeks go pink, and I want to high five myself for the cleverness of my idea. I feel a bit uncomfortable pretending. Lying, actually, but the only other option is to admit it was me, so lying it is.

"Look," she points to the chocolates. "It's like they know me."

"Have you eaten any yet?"

"No. I wanted to show you first."

That statement causes a strange tightening in my chest.

"I spent the day wrangling male egos." She rolls her eyes. As the lone female in the band, she does a lot of this. "So, by the time I got home, I was cranky and exhausted. But then this arrived." A shy smile. "I've never had a secret admirer before." Her eyes are bright, her happiness like a drug. There's no way I can stop now. I'm already planning my next Rosie surprise.

掀掀

Secret Nigel has been busy. Two deliveries a week for the last three weeks. At first, I stuck with the red roses and chocolate hearts combo, until Rosie said something about SN being predictable. This engendered a small moment of panic, when I realised Real Nigel was bleeding into Secret Nigel. Real Nigel is predictable and boring. But Secret Nigel is sexy and exciting, a perfect match for Rosie's wild creative spirit. Rosie seems quite taken with Secret Nigel. Real Nigel, however, is still firmly in the friendzone with no hope of escape.

Rosie walks in with the latest delivery, a rose made entirely of chocolate with a big red bow. She places it on the kitchen bench and starts to read the card. I attempt to peer over her shoulder, but she slaps me away. "It's private."

Her cheeks darken as she reads. In this note, Secret Nigel tells her he's heard her sing, and how much he loves her voice.

I frown. Something uncomfortably like jealousy stabs through me. It never occurred to me that I would be competing with a fictional version of myself – and losing.

"Do you think he'll want to meet sometime?" Her voice is hopeful. "I really want to meet him."

I shrug casually, turning so she can't see my face. *Crap.* In the excitement of conceiving my *Win Rosie with Chocolate* plan, I failed to consider all the ramifications of said plan. Like how this thing was going to end.

If I stop sending things, she'll think I've lost interest. But she wants to meet... *Christ.* What the hell am I going to do? I can't string her along forever. But the thought of her being mad – or worse – disappointed, when she finds out its me and not the romantic charmer she's imagined, turns my stomach.

I make a secret email address and attach it to the next delivery, which is Rosie's name spelled out in chocolate letters, in a gold, rectangular box.

She responds immediately, thanking me for all the chocolate surprises, saying how much they meant to her and how she would really like to meet me. Well, not me – Secret Nigel.

My gut churns with nausea. There's only one thing I can do. And she's going to hate me.

ଔଓ

I wait in the shadows outside the restaurant until I see Rosie go in. Then, after a few moments, follow. My stomach clenches in sick fear, as if I'm going to the firing squad.

When Rosie sees me approaching the table, her eyes widen in surprise. Then she frowns. "What are you doing here?"

I take a deep breath, and slide into the seat where Secret Nigel is supposed to be sitting. I clear my throat, twice. "I ...uh, have to tell you something."

Her eyes narrow.

Oh God. "It was me, the secret admirer."

There's a silence so deep it's like everyone in the restaurant is holding their breath.

Rosie stares at me, eyes flashing. "What? Were you sitting there laughing at me the whole time while I made a fool of myself? Is this a joke to you?"

The slight wobble in her voice kills me. Her eyes have gone shiny. *Crap.*

"What? No, of course not."

"I thought you were my friend."

"I am."

"You *lied.*"

The word hangs between us like an undetonated grenade.

"I... not exactly."

The disgusted shake of her head tells me she's just thrown me into the *Liars and Deniers* box with Dylan.

Rosie pushes out her chair.

My pulse doubles in speed. "*Wait!* Please."

She sighs heavily and pulls her chair back in. "Truth, or I'm out of here."

I swallow hard. "I didn't know how else to tell you how I feel. I'm no good at this kind of thing. Apart from my identity, everything I said was true. I love you."

Her eyes widen but I press on. "I pretended to be someone else because I thought you'd never want me as I am."

"Why would you think that?"

"Because I'm not cool or brave, like you. I'm an awkward dork. You're gorgeous and amazing and wonderful and I'm just – me. But I want you so much, I can hardly stand it." My voice cracks. "You're everything to me, and I'm so sorry I hurt you."

I hang my head in abject misery. A firing squad would be preferable to seeing the hurt in her eyes. Hurt that I put there.

When I look up, she's watching me with an expression I can't read.

"What does SN stand for?"

Heat floods my cheeks. "Secret Nigel."

Her lips twitch. "Well, Secret Nigel, you are an idiot..."

My shoulders sag.

"...if you think I would prefer a made-up guy to the real you."

I stare at her in confusion.

"Why didn't you tell me how you felt? I thought you only wanted to be friends."

"I thought you'd reject me."

Rosie's eyes soften. "Oh, Nige. You're the sweetest guy I know. And in case you haven't noticed, sweet things are my weakness."

My stupid heart splutters with hope. Either that or I'm having a heart attack.

Warm, chocolate eyes look deep into mine, as if she can see every part of me and likes what she sees. She shoots me a slow, sexy smile.

"Well, at least now I don't feel so bad about all the inappropriate fantasies I was having about you."

"You were?"

She stares at my lips and my whole body explodes with longing. "You know, you're really hot when you're doing that whole conscientious dentist thing."

All I know is that she said 'me' and 'hot' in the same sentence. But I have to be clear. "I'm serious about this. I don't want a casual thing. I want you for real, for keeps."

"I know Nigels are forever, not just for Christmas." Then she takes my hand in hers and says in a more serious tone. "I'm crazy about you, too." She shakes her head with a smile. "If I'd known you felt this way, I would have jumped on you months ago."

Rosie slips out of her chair then and motions to me to do the same. Her arms slide around my neck and my hands grip her waist. Then her lips brush mine, a soft slow caress that sparks an inferno of need. We kiss slow and deep, and everything melts away until there's only her and me and this exquisite thing blooming between us.

Her soft curves press against me, and I pull her closer, wanting all of her, wanting everything.

When we finally pull apart, Rosie's cheeks are flushed, her lips plump and moist from our kiss. Then I realise everyone in the restaurant is staring at us and the waiting staff are all grinning.

My cheeks burn as we sit down again.

"We *are* staying for dinner, aren't we?" Rosie's voice is hopeful.

"Of course."

"Good." She grins. "Because they have chocolate torte for dessert."

"You want to share?"

"Of course not. Do you know me at all?"

I laugh so hard I have to wipe my eyes because that response is pure Rosie. Every cell of my body fizzes with unadulterated joy. I take her hand, entwining our fingers, while the smiling waitress takes our order.

SPICY BITES

Want to try something a little spicier?

Why not try our Spicy Bites Anthology?

SPICY BITES 2021:
DENIM

Spicy Bites anthologies can be purchased from the
Romance Writers of Australia store

http://romanceaustralia.com/shop/

COMING IN 2022

Sweet Treats

Think of all those yummy treats that make you feel good, or that you might get or make for your loved ones.

The theme for 2022 is

Ice Cream

Find full details on the Romance Writers of Australia website

https://romanceaustralia.com/contests-overview/sweet-treats-anthology/

Previous Little Gems and Sweet Treats anthologies can be purchased from the Romance Writers of Australia store

https://romanceaustralia.com/shop/

ABOUT THE AUTHORS

Toni D'Alia

Toni D'Alia writes contemporary romance novels, short stories, and children's books. She worked as a teacher for a number of years, but made the change from teaching to writing and discovered her dream career.

When she isn't writing, Toni loves spending quality time with her family. She enjoys reading, movie nights, pyjama days, and catching up with good friends.

Cordelia Fox

A jack-of-all trades, Cordelia Fox has worked as a nurse and a midwife; in big cities, rural New Zealand, and remote Australia. She is also a trained librarian. Currently, she teaches History at a secondary school in the deep south of New Zealand.

In her stories, Cordelia loves to draw on her personal wealth of experiences. She enjoys writing steamy romances with strong, articulate heroines. In the future she may start (and even complete) a PhD in History. Alternatively, she may work on her Spanish and go and live in Cuba. Cordelia has written 1½ novels and several short stories.

Arietta Richmond

Arietta Richmond has been a compulsive writer all her life. She is fascinated by history, and historical novels are her favourite reading.

Her writing covers a wide range, some under other pennames, and she has written more than 80 novels, 49 (so far) being Regency Romance. They include a number of series – 'The Derbyshire Set', 'His Majesty's Hounds', the Nettlefold Chronicles and the Elbury Bouquet – as well as some standalone novels, and she has many more books planned. She likes to travel, to see in person the places where history happened.

Discover more at http://www.ariettarichmond.com and receive two free stories.

Stephanie Ashton

Overheard conversations and opening paragraphs of stories have filled Stephanie's notebooks since she was ten. A former international flight attendant, she's inspired by favourite destinations and the feeling of coming home. When not writing she adds to her baking bucket list, tries new food and discovers destinations closer to home. She lives in Melbourne with her partner and daughter, and no pets, yet. Say hello at:

https://www.stephanieashtonwrites.com

https://www.facebook.com/StephanieAshtonWrites

https://www.instagram.com/stephanieashtonwrites

Frances Dall'Alba

As an aspiring author of romance and women's fiction, Frances Dall'Alba loves nothing more than losing herself in a good romance. She's all about helping you forget the housework, or the bus to work you're going to miss, if you don't put the book down now! She's devoted to giving her readers an emotional, yet satisfying ride, with a love story that'll melt your heart and keep the pages turning right until the end.

When she isn't writing, Frances is climbing mountains, searching for waterfalls and swimming across lakes. She loves to exercise, agrees it's not fair she has to cook dinner every night, and never notices dust on the furniture. She lives with her husband in tropical Far North Queensland, and uses her great baking skills to tempt her three daughters to visit home as often as they can.

Caroline Deness

Caroline loves reading romance, humour and happy endings—who doesn't? She started writing when she ran out of books by her then favourite author, Janet Evanovich. After all, there are only so many times a year a person can reread Georgette Heyer or Jane Austen books. Even more perfect was when Caroline discovered modern Regency Romance. She has a story in the RWAus 2019 Little Gems Anthology, *Tiger's Eye*, titled *The Tiger's Eyes*. A big thank you to her 'avid readers of the genre'. Find another story at carolinedeness.com.

Visit her website

http://francesdallalba.wixsite.com/francesdallalba for all her writing achievements.

Louisa Duval

Louisa currently works in education and lives between Brisbane and Ballandean, in Queensland's Granite Belt region, with her husband, two kids and a lazy, fat cattle dog/Kelpie X. She loves the local wine and the volunteer firefighters who keep the region safe.

Louisa has worked in radio as a correspondent for the Granite Belt and is a graduate of The University of Queensland's writing, editing and publishing program. You can find her on Facebook, Instagram and Twitter, and sign up for her newsletter via her website: https://louisaduval.com

Amy Hutton

Amy Hutton is a writer of contemporary romance, often with a spooky twist. A member of RWA since 2018, Amy was thrilled to be published in the Sweet Treats anthology in 2020, and again in the 2021.

When not writing, she's an award-winning television producer, Disneyland aficionado and devoted movie buff, with a particular fondness for romance and horror who enjoys attending pop culture conventions in Australia and the United States. A proud owner of a dog called Buffy, Amy is also the custodian of two yabbies named Sebastian and Thermidor.

You can find Amy @AmyHuttonAuthor on Twitter and Instagram.

Kylie Jacobs

Kylie Jacobs is an aspiring author from South Australia who writes stories in different genres – from humorous tales that feature older, female protagonists to contemporary stories with unexpected twists and turns.

As well as her love for writing short stories and novels, she recently placed as a finalist in two separate LA screenplay competitions for a comedic screenplay. Now her four children are older, she looks forward to being able to focus on her writing career. Follow her on Facebook or Instagram @kyliejacobswriter

J A MacNally

Jan is addicted to writing, starting with the first Science Fiction story she penned while still in primary school. With careers in both teaching and government, she's had autobiographical and fiction short stories published, including in RWA's 2020 and 2021 *Spicy Bites* anthologies. She has written countless articles and reviews for online websites, newsletters and her own blog. She's a costumed member of the *Star Wars* 501st Legion Knightfall Garrison, reads mainly chick-lit and paranormal genres, and loves collecting literary or cinematic spin-offs relating to Jane Austen, who first hooked her on literature. Jan's blog can be found at:

https://suchreviewsaboutnothing.wordpress.com/author/suchreviews aboutnothing/

Instagram: https://www.instagram.com/karls.girl/

Fiona M Marsden

Fiona M Marsden started as an avid reader. She was late in finding romance novels, but once found, they became an addiction. Considering she wrote poetry and stories from a young age, it was only logical that the next step would be to write her own romances. Her favourite genres are contemporary and historical. She recently started writing rural romance reflecting her long years of country living in regional Australia. Fiona is a hybrid author with several independently published works and upcoming contracts with Escape Publishing and Tule Publishing.

Twitter & Instagram: @fionammarsden

Facebook Author Page:

https://www.facebook.com/PrincessFionaMarsden

Web: www.fionamarsden.com

Clare Miles

Clare Miles can't remember a time when she didn't love reading, and growing up in a big loud family it was the perfect escape. Years later her household isn't quite as noisy, but her love of reading and escape has never diminished, nor the desire to write her very own happily-ever-afters. She's absolutely thrilled to be part of the Sweet Treats Anthology and hopes you enjoy Pippa and Jed's story, the first time she's moved away from her city dwelling heroes and heroines and gone bush!

You can find her on Instagram as Clare Miles Author, or at www.facebook.com/clare.miles.7106 or in her favourite chocolate shop!

Valerie Miller

Valerie is a secondary teacher and a writer. She lives in Brisbane, Australia with her husband and daughter, after moving from Sydney four years ago. Valerie is currently completing a Master of Letters in Creative Writing and writing her first novel. She is the daughter of Italian migrants and enjoys writing short stories that have an Italian cultural and family focus. Her dog Mischa and cats, Daisy and Miss Lilly, are her writing companions. You will always find a novel and notebook filled with ideas and observations, tucked away in her handbag.

You can connect with Valerie at:

https://www.valeriegmiller.com

Georgia Moore

Georgia writes contemporary romances featuring strong friendships and food as a love language, and SFF novels with plenty of action and heat. She's currently writing a sci-fi romance. In 2020, her short stories featured in RWA's Sweet Treats and Spicy Bites anthologies.

When not consuming copious amounts of pop-culture, Georgia can be found attempting a new cake recipe, singing in a choir, or being overly competitive at board games.

Follow Georgia on Twitter, Facebook and Instagram

@GMooreWriter

Kristin Silk

Kristin Silk loves weaving words and worlds. She lives with her family and a small but squeaky, furry tyrant, Martha the guinea pig, who believes she is alpha of the household. (We don't have the heart to correct her.)

In 2019 and 2020 Kristin placed second in RWAus Spicy Bites competitions and her stories appear in the *Masks* and *Leather* anthologies, respectively. Her story, Sleeping Beauty and the Librarian, won the 2020 Valerie Parv award. She writes fantasy, paranormal and contemporary romance.

She can be found haunting cyberspace at KristinSilkWriter (Facebook), @kristin.silk (Instagram) and @SilkKristin (Twitter).